I enthusiastically signed out of chat and switched to the *When in Rome* website. It took forever to load. And *then* I had to sign into my blog and wait all over again for the main page to come up. One thing was for sure: at this rate, I'd never get a vlog posted. I'd die and fossilize before the connection would upload any photos, let alone a video. A short post would have to do. I could write something about my first impression of Costa Rica. I composed the opening sentence in my head as I waited for the blog page to load. Maybe that's why it took me a moment to process what I saw on the page when it finally did.

My blog had already been updated, only not by me.

OTHER BOOKS YOU MAY ENJOY

LIGHTS, CAMERA, CASSIDY

episode three:
Hacked

by LINDA GERBER

PUFFIN BOOKS
An Imprint of Penguin Group (USA) Inc.

PUFFIN BOOKS

Published by the Penguin Group

Penguin Young Readers Group, 345 Hudson Street, New York, New York 10014, U.S.A.

Penguin Group (Canada), 90 Eglinton Avenue East, Suite 700, Toronto, Ontario, Canada M4P 2Y3
(a division of Pearson Penguin Canada Inc.)

Penguin Books Ltd, 80 Strand, London WC2R 0RL, England

Penguin Ireland, 25 St Stephen's Green, Dublin 2, Ireland (a division of Penguin Books Ltd)

Penguin Group (Australia), 250 Camberwell Road, Camberwell, Victoria 3124, Australia
(a division of Pearson Australia Group Pty Ltd)

Penguin Books India Pvt Ltd, 11 Community Centre,
Panchsheel Park, New Delhi - 110 017, India

Penguin Group (NZ), 67 Apollo Drive, Rosedale, Auckland 0632, New Zealand
(a division of Pearson New Zealand Ltd)

Penguin Books (South Africa) (Pty) Ltd, 24 Sturdee Avenue,
Rosebank, Johannesburg 2196, South Africa

Penguin Books Ltd, Registered Offices: 80 Strand, London WC2R 0RL, England

First published in the United States of America by Puffin Books,
a member of Penguin Young Readers Group, 2012

1 3 5 7 9 10 8 6 4 2

Copyright © Linda Gerber, 2012
All rights reserved

LIBRARY OF CONGRESS CATALOGING-IN-PUBLICATION DATA IS AVAILABLE

Puffin Books ISBN 978-0-14-241816-1

Design by Theresa Evangelista
Text set in Adobe Caslon regular

Printed in the United States of America

ALWAYS LEARNING   PEARSON

For Lily. Welcome to twelve!

ACKNOWLEDGMENTS: Special thanks to everyone who helped make this book a reality; to my family for respecting the closed office door (and loving me despite my crazy moments); to Mama Tica for teaching me about *pura vida*; to Elaine Spencer for supreme agenting and friendship; to Kristin Gilson for editorial wisdom and guidence; and to Theresa Evangelista, whose cover work I adore. I owe you all big time!

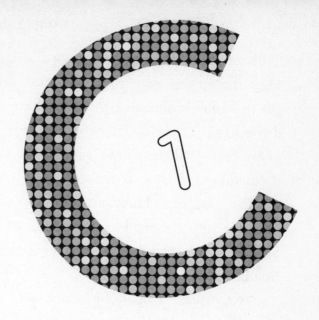

Travel tip: Most people come to Costa
Rica to relax, so please don't be in a hurry.

For my last vocab test, I learned at least three definitions for the word *irony*. But it wasn't until weeks later, when I was riding shotgun with Bayani on a winding dirt road in Costa Rica, that I fully understood the meaning.

He had cranked up the truck's stereo as high as it would go with his favorite classic rock CD and was drumming his hands on the steering wheel to the pounding beat. At the top of his lungs he shouted along with "Born to Be Wild" . . . as he drove at the heart-racing pace of about five miles per hour.

Even more ironic: I had jumped at the chance to ride from the airport with Bayani because I couldn't wait to get to Monteverde and I thought he would be the fastest driver. As it turns out, the truck he was driving was the one carrying all the show's equipment, so he had to take it careful—and slow. It wasn't so bad when we were on the Pan-American Highway, but the minute we turned off onto the unpaved roads, forget about it. The other three SUVs carrying the rest of the crew passed us before the first bridge.

"Aw, c'mon!" I bounced in my seat. "Can't we go any faster?"

He turned the music down long enough to give me his (terrible) Joker impression. "Why so ssserious, Cassidy?"

"I just want to get there."

Bayani laughed and cranked the music back up. "Relax!" he shouted over the heavy bass beat. "Don't be in such a hurry to get where you're going that you can't enjoy the ride!"

Sure. Easy for him to say. His best friend-slash-crush wasn't waiting for him at the end of the ride. Mine was. I hadn't seen Logan since Spain; I think that gave me the right to be anxious.

Not that I'd ever tell Bayani that. He'd just use it in his arsenal of Tease Cassidy ammunition.

Bayani's the "fixer" with my mom and dad's cable travel show, *When in Rome*. He's the guy who makes all the practical arrangements for the show when we go on location—secures reservations, lines up the local guides, gets the necessary permits, and hauls equipment. He takes care of everything in advance so that when the rest of the crew shows up, all they have to do is shoot the episode. Bayani's been with the show so long, he's become like a big brother to me . . . with all that goes with the role, like being a huge tease.

But I wasn't going to let his teasing or anything else spoil this trip. Logan was here! That was all that mattered.

Logan and I go way back, to when the show first started. His dad's *When in Rome*'s producer, my mom and dad are the stars, so Logan and I both traveled with the show. We were the only kids in the group, so we became best friends by default. For years, we were inseparable—until his mom decided it was time for him to "stop ladding about" and settle down with her in Ireland.

After that, I didn't see Logan for two years. I didn't hear from him, either. He never wrote, never called. And then suddenly, there he was at our shoot in Spain.

The years we were apart changed some things—we were both a couple of years older, both a little taller (though Logan gained several inches on me), and his voice had gotten deeper. But in many ways, we picked right up where we left off, as if Logan had never been away. We still talked, we still joked around, we still fought; we were still best friends. It wasn't until it was time to leave Spain that I realized I liked him as something more. By then, it was too late, because I had gotten myself shipped off to the States to stay with my gramma.

Logan and I IMed and video chatted the whole time I was away, but it wasn't the same as being there in person. Now I was moments away from seeing him again, and I couldn't get there fast enough.

I turned down the stereo and nudged Bayani's arm. "How much farther?"

"Not far. We got about twenty minutes to Monteverde, then another fifteen to the farm."

Not far? Thirty-five minutes hardly qualified as not far. And was he talking thirty-five minutes at the speed the rest of the crew was traveling, or at the snail's pace he was driving?

Oh, and the farm? Here's another lovely bit of irony for you . . . when the network invited me to come to Costa Rica to film some kid-friendly spots for my mom and dad's show, I'd been at my gramma's farm in Ohio for nearly a month and a half and was dying to escape. Don't get me wrong. I love my gramma, and I love going to visit her between shows, but I grew up on the road. Staying in one place for so long was torture. And let's face it, farm life? Not so exciting. So here I had left one farm only to travel all the way to Costa Rica and land on another one.

But it didn't matter. *Logan was here!* We could be staying at a monastery for all I cared.

• • • • •

As the road wound higher up the steep hillside, misty tendrils of fog drifted by the truck. *No, not fog*, I reminded myself, *clouds*. Always-present clouds. The forests of Monteverde were called cloud forests for that reason.

From the valley, we hadn't been able to see much of the mountain because it had been swallowed by the clouds. Now we were driving into them, bumping and swaying over the rutted dirt road. The mist grew thicker and denser until the road, the trees, and everything ahead of us faded to gray.

Bayani slowed the truck even more and rolled his window down a crack. "Smells like rain again," he said.

The air that whistled in through the opening was earthy and damp. It was also cooler than the air in San Jose had been. I shivered and grabbed the Ohio State hoodie from my backpack and slipped it on. I didn't think I would need it when Gramma gave it to me as a good-bye present, but now I was glad I had it. "Has it been raining a lot?" I asked Bayani. "Is that going to mess with the shoot schedule?"

"Ooh." He slid me a look and mocked me with his eyebrows. "Look at you being Miss Diva, concerning yourself with schedules and all."

I smacked his arm. "Shut up."

Of course he'd rib me about the diva thing. Apparently, when I had been in Greece filming a kids' travel special, one of the American tabloids said I was copping a diva attitude because I "turned up my nose" at my "hottie costar" Nikos Kouropoulos. They claimed I thought I was too good for him. Which is ironic, because the European tabloids made it sound like the two of us were taking a ride on the *Love Boat*.

What none of them understood—and what I wasn't about to tell them because it was none of their business— was that (a) the whole time we were on the yacht, I was trying to set Nikos up with my friend Zoe, and (b) the only guy I was interested in was Logan. Still, somehow it got out that I was being a diva—just the kind of thing Bayani loved to have in his arsenal.

"If the weather interferes," he continued loftily, "we can move your ten o'clock to eleven and your eleven o'clock to twelve thirty. I'll have my people call your people and we'll pencil it in."

"You're such an idiot."

"And you are, if I may quote, 'a rising young star in the galaxy of reality TV.' Wow, does that sound wrong."

I smacked him again, and he hunched his shoulder away from me. "Hey. No assaulting the driver."

"No insulting the passenger," I shot back.

"What insult? I'm just repeating what *Celeb Style* said."

"With a little personal commentary at the end."

"Ah, c'mon." He reached over and ruffled my hair like I was three instead of thirteen. "You know you're my favorite starlet."

"Stop with the starlet stuff," I warned him, smoothing my bangs. Without thinking, I flipped down the visor so I could check my hair in the mirror. I didn't want Logan to see me for the first time in months looking like I had just woken up.

Bayani burst out laughing, and I slapped the visor back up against the truck's ceiling.

"Ha!" he crowed, waggling a finger at me. "Who's not a diva?"

I huffed and slid down in my seat, arms folded tight across my chest. But even as I muttered to myself and stared out the window, I couldn't hide my smile. It was good to be back.

Just before we reached the farm, Finca Calderón, it started to rain. No, that sounds much too tame. More like it started to pour, all at once, like someone had turned on a faucet above us full blast. The dirt road melted into slick mud beneath the truck, running in rivulets down the hill as if it might wash away altogether. The windshield wipers *thwapped* frantically back and forth, but they couldn't keep up with the deluge. Water cascaded down the glass in sheets, turning the world into a wavy, soft-focus kaleidoscope.

It was through the kaleidoscope that I saw the cows. Three ginger and white and one black and white huddled together at the base of one of the trees, stoically blinking against the rain. I was never so happy to see cows in my life. We were staying at a dairy farm after all, which meant . . . "We're close?"

Bayani nodded. "Just over this rise."

Suddenly, I was nervous. Not scared-nervous, but excited-nervous. In just a few more minutes, I'd be with Logan. There were so many things I wanted to say to him. So much time I wanted to make up. I couldn't wait to see him. If it hadn't been raining so hard, I might have been tempted to jump out of the slow-moving truck and run the rest of the way.

Bayani must have noticed me getting antsy. "Can't wait to get in front of the camera again, huh?" he ribbed.

"You know it." I fluffed my hair and blew him a kiss and left it at that. The last thing I was going to do was tell him how excited I was to see Logan. If Bayani knew, I'd never hear the end of it.

Fortunately, he didn't have time for any follow-through. Just as he'd said, a big wooden sign announcing Finca Calderón stood at the crest of the hill. We turned onto a long dirt driveway that—if possible—was even more hole pocked and rutted than the road. A couple of rustic-looking houses and a cluster of outbuildings waited for us at the end of the driveway.

"I'll let you out by the door," Bayani told me, "and pull the truck into the shed. We can unload when the rain lets up."

It didn't look like that was going to be any time soon.

Rain pelted against the windows as hard as ever. "Do you have an umbrella?" I asked hopefully.

"Naw. I'll be fine," Bayani said. "I'm not worried about getting wet." He paused for a moment and then gave me one of those fake, wide-eyed, just-now-understanding faces. "Oh, you mean for you. No. I'm afraid not. That would be why I'm dropping you at the door."

By then he had pulled the truck to a stop in front of the larger house. Not more than ten steps from the driveway, a porch with a vine-covered arbor ran the length of the building, but the way it was raining, ten steps was enough to get soaking wet. Maybe if I protected my head with my backpack . . .

"Get out already," Bayani said. "Unless you want to walk with me from the shed." He pointed to an outbuilding several yards from the house.

"No, this is good." I resisted the urge to check the mirror one last time (what good would it do?) and pushed the door open.

I was right. It didn't matter how fast I ran. By the time I made it under the protection of the arbor, my hair was plastered to my head and my sopping clothes clung to me. Not quite the look I was going for when Logan saw me again for the first time, but what could I do? I squished up to the front entrance, shivering. A sign by the door said in Spanish and English, *¡ENTRA!* COME IN! I pushed my dripping hair out of my face, squared my shoulders, and walked through the doorway.

The lodge didn't look nearly as rustic inside as it had on the outside. A wrought-iron chandelier hung in the two-story entrance, and the wood floors held the kind of mellow gleam that comes with age and a lot of care. In the huge center room a fire crackled in a stone-lined fireplace. Woodsmoke mingled with a homey spice-and-floral smell that was both exotic and familiar at the same time.

It looked like a regular meet-and-greet was going on in the big room. My tutor, Victoria, our makeup guy, Daniel, and a woman I guessed was our new techie were sitting on the leather couches in front of the fireplace. My dad had mentioned gaining a new crew member while I was gone. Britt, I think her name was. She was supposed to be a computer genius or something. From where I was standing, she looked more like a flirt, batting her eyelashes at a couple of dark-haired guys I didn't recognize and laughing behind her hand, all dainty and coy.

Across the room, my mom and dad stood with Logan's dad, talking to some blonde lady I'd never seen before. Huh. Dad never said anything about *two* new crew members. But before I could give her much thought, the blonde lady, my mom, my dad, and the entire room faded away when I finally saw Logan, sprawled in an oversize wingback chair in the corner, reading a book. My breath caught, just as it always did when I saw him. And I froze on the spot.

For months, all I'd been able to think about was seeing Logan again, but now that the moment had come, I was suddenly unsure. How should I make my big entrance? Act casual? Call out to him? Sneak up and smack the book from his hands? That last one would be the most fun. I started toward him, but before I could take two steps, Daniel's voice cut through the chatter.

"Ah, there she is!"

Everything went quiet for a heartbeat before picking up again. So much for sneaking.

Victoria called hello from her seat near the fireplace and stood to make her way toward me. Daniel followed close behind. My eyes skipped over them both to where Logan was still sitting. Only now he was watching me. My face suddenly went hot, and I forced a smile, waving to him. His smile looked a lot more genuine when he waved back. That's all it took for hot chills to ripple through my stomach.

"We thought you got lost," Victoria said when she reached me.

I reluctantly pulled my attention away from Logan. "Not lost," I said. "Just slow."

"And soaked!" Daniel plucked at the sleeve of my hoodie. "Look at you."

"It's raining," I told him.

"Well, come in by the fire and dry off." Victoria bustled me from the entry into the main room. "I'll introduce you to our *tico* friends."

"*Tico?*"

"That's what they call the locals," Daniel explained, "on account of how they talk."

Which didn't explain a thing as far as I was concerned. "How they talk?"

"Their speech," Victoria said. "Costa Ricans are known for adding the diminutive '*-tico*' suffix to words, hence the name *tico*. Or *tica* for the feminine."

"Okay, I have no idea what you just said," I told her, "but I bet we'll talk about it in our lessons." She always did find a way to add stuff about our host country to our studies wherever we traveled.

"That and a whole treasure of *tiquismos*," she said, smiling.

"Tiki-what?"

"*Tiquismos*. Colloquialisms."

"Later," Daniel said, "but now we need to introduce you to our new friend Marco." He took my arm to steer me over. "He'll be our *tico* guide while we're here. You'll love him. The guy's a gas."

"Oh. Uh . . ." I stole a quick peek to where Logan was still sitting. *Why* was he still sitting? Shouldn't he have come over to say hi by now? Sure, I had stopped to talk with Victoria and Daniel, but if it had been me sitting there and

Logan had walked into the room, I would have jumped up and run straight over to him.

". . . met Britt yet, have you?" Victoria was asking.

I blinked back to the present. "I'm sorry?"

"Britt," Victoria repeated. "She joined us while you were in Ohio."

"Come on," Daniel prodded. "I'll introduce you to her, too."

"Sure." I forced a smile. "That would be great."

Daniel presented me to Marco first. He looked pleasant enough, with friendly eyes and a full, wide mouth that broke easily into a smile. He'd been talking to Britt, but he excused himself and stood as we approached. She smiled stiffly and pushed to her feet as well.

"This," Daniel told him, "is Cassidy." And then to me, "Cassidy, may I present Marco. And our newest crew member, Britt."

Britt murmured a greeting I could barely hear, but before I could answer her, Marco took my hand and bent over it like I was some kind of royalty.

"Ah, *la chica moda*," he said, his dark eyes laughing. "*Con mucho gusto*. It is a pleasure."

I groaned and pulled my hand away so I could swat Daniel. "You had to tell him?"

La chica moda was a nickname the tabloids had given me in Spain. It means "the stylish girl." And since I must have looked like a drowned kitten with my wet, stringy hair and rain-soaked clothes, I could see why Marco found the name funny. Thanks a lot, Daniel. I pulled myself up taller than I felt and nodded back at Marco. *"Gracias,"* I said. "Thanks. It's nice to meet you, too."

Marco asked the usual polite questions: how was the flight, how did I like Costa Rica so far, what kind of stuff did I like to do—that sort of thing. I tried to give equally polite answers, but my eyes kept wandering over to Logan. Maybe he was waiting for me to come to him?

Finally, Victoria saved me. "Well," she said, nodding first to Marco and then to Britt, "we didn't mean to interrupt, but we wanted to give Cassidy the chance to meet you."

"No problem," Britt said, suddenly all smiles.

"Our pleasure," Marco said. *"Ahí nos vidrios,* Cassidy. I will see you later."

With the necessary pleasantries out of the way, Victoria pulled me aside. She nodded toward Logan. "Go on."

"Thank you," I whispered, and turned to start across the room.

Which was when my dad called out to me. "Cassidy! Come on over. There's someone here I'd like you to meet."

I trudged to where he and Mom were standing with Cavin and the mystery lady. Logan glanced up at me as I passed him and gave me a little shrug and a half smile. I didn't know what that was supposed to mean, but I shrugged in return anyway. My shrug meant, *I have no idea how I'm supposed to act right now.*

"Cassidy." Dad pulled my attention back to him. "This is Elizabeth Ricketson from the network."

Ah. I should have known. She did have that polished media-executive look—tailored clothes, understated makeup, no-nonsense hair, a smile that was a little too broad to be genuine.

"Hi, Cassidy," she said, stretching her well-manicured hand toward me. "You may call me Liz."

I shook her hand the way my mom had taught me to do, with a firm but gentle grip and steady eye contact. "Pleased to meet you," I said.

"And I'm delighted to meet you. I'm looking forward to working with you and Logan on the junior features."

"She's the producer for the promotional spots you kids will be filming for this episode," Mom interpreted.

I nodded and slipped another look at Logan . . . and my heart dropped. He was scowling now, looking the other way.

"We're very energized about the potential for this project," Liz said. "We think it's going to do very well for us."

"We'll talk more about it once ye've had a chance to settle in," Cavin said. Then to the adults, "If you'll excuse me, I'll see to the room assignments."

I jumped at the chance to excuse myself as well. "If you

don't need me," I said, backing away, "I'd like to say hi to Logan. It was nice meeting you, Liz."

"We'll chat soon," she promised. "We have a lot to talk about. Very exciting stuff."

When I finally managed to break away, I hurried over to Logan before anyone else could stop me.

He set his book aside and stood as I got closer. "Hi, Cass" was all he said.

That's it. Monotone. No smile. Nothing. It's like I was just seeing him again after being in another room instead of another country. All those weeks of missing him, I had imagined this moment much differently. In my perfect scenario, there was hugging involved. I almost worked up the nerve to give him a quick hug then, but to tell the truth, I wanted him to be the one who made the first move. Plus, I was suddenly feeling a lot shyer than I should have felt with my best friend. I hugged my soggy arms around myself instead and just said hi back.

"How was your flight?" he asked politely.

I shrugged. My travels weren't exactly what I had hoped we'd talk about. Not that I had the conversation mapped out or anything, but I thought as best friends we were beyond small talk. "Fine, I guess," I told him. "How are you? Is everything okay?"

"Yeah. Why?"

I hugged my arms tighter and hunched my shoulders.

"I don't know."

He motioned for me to sit in his wingback chair, and he took the tooled leather ottoman in front of it. "You mean with Da," he said in a low voice.

Is it bad that a gigantic swell of relief washed over me? Here I was reading all sorts of things into Logan not coming to say hello, but if there was tension with his dad, he could have simply been distracted. Maybe I didn't have to worry. I almost let myself smile, but that probably wouldn't have looked very supportive, so I showed him my best concerned frown instead. "Right. Your dad. What's going on?"

This time he shrugged. "No big deal. It's just this project thing."

"Uh-huh?" I had no idea what project he was talking about, but I leaned forward, nodding, the very picture of understanding and sympathy.

"Nothing."

"No, tell me."

"I don't know." He glanced quickly over his shoulder and lowered his voice. "I mean, you probably get the same thing from your mum and dad all the time. Like what happened with you and Mateo in Spain. I just wish he'd ask, you know?"

Now I was totally lost. Mateo was my dad's old college buddy's son. When we were in Valencia, Mateo had gotten roped into doing a bunch of on-camera background shots with me. But what did that have to do with Logan? "I don't—"

"These 'spots,' or whatever you call them," he said, waving a hand in the air. "It was never, 'Logan, would you like to do them?' It was 'Logan, you're *going* to do them,' and 'We need it for the show.'"

My heart dropped right down to the polished wood floor. Not good. *I* was the one who had suggested Logan do the promo spots with me, not his dad. And "suggested" isn't exactly the right word, either; I'd told Cavin it was a condition of my coming to Costa Rica. I'd figured if Logan and I were both working on the spots, we'd have more time to spend together. I hadn't ever considered that Logan might not want to do them.

"I don't know," I said weakly. "It could be fun."

He shook his head, and his dark hair fell into his eyes. He pushed it away impatiently. "Not my thing."

The tone of his voice hit me straight in the gut. Dismissive. Disgusted. As if being in those spots with me would be beneath him.

"It's not so bad," I said, a bit defensively. "You might like it."

"Are you serious? The cheesy lines? The fake enthusiasm? No, thanks."

"You could try it for a day. It might not be so—"

"No. No way. I don't want to be some idiot pretending for the camera like—"

"Like what I do," I cut in.

"That's not what I meant."

"It's okay. I get it. You're too good for that kind of thing."

"Cass, stop." He reached for my hand, but I pulled it away. He didn't want to do the spots? Fine. Not everyone was comfortable on camera. But he didn't have to disrespect what I did. What my parents did.

"I should go get changed," I said, standing. "Wet clothes suck."

"Cassidy . . ."

I walked away, and it felt like my heart was breaking up, dissolving, just like those roads in the rain. I'd been so excited about seeing Logan again. I had daydreamed how it would be, the two of us spending every day together. Now I was wet, I was miserable, and I wished I'd never left Gramma's farm. At least when I was still there, I could pretend Logan liked me as much as I liked him.

Maybe I really was an idiot, like he said.

All the guest quarters were nestled

around the circular balcony that made up the lodge's second floor. I had my own room, if you could call it that, right next to my mom and dad's. The space wasn't much larger than a closet, with a narrow bed pushed up against the wall and a small dresser squeezed in under an even smaller window. The sleeping arrangements were a little tight, my mom explained, but everyone could spread out in the common areas, like the kitchen and the dining room and the big open room downstairs. Family-style, my dad called it.

"They offered to let the three of us stay in the smaller bungalow," Mom added, "in the casita. We would have privacy there, but we thought it might be more fun to be where the action is."

Action. Great. Usually, I would be the one begging to stay where everyone else was so I wouldn't miss anything, but all I could think of was that Logan would be staying in the lodge, too, and now I'd have to be on guard to avoid him. I wouldn't want him to have to pretend to be nice to me.

"Well, we'll leave you to it," Dad said.

Mom hesitated before pulling my door closed as they left. "You'll feel better once you've unpacked," she said.

If only it was that easy.

When I was in Greece, I met a girl named Zoe, who worked on our yacht. She had a serious crush on Nikos, the guy who was doing the travel special with me. I did all I could to push Zoe and Nikos together, and it worked. In the meantime, Zoe and I became good friends. She was the one person who knew all about Logan and me. Maybe she could tell me what to do about our disastrous reunion.

I dropped onto the bed and pulled out my phone to text her, but there were no connectivity bars in the corner of the screen. Just to be sure, I tested for a ringtone. Nothing. "You've got to be kidding me." I held the phone up higher. Climbed onto the bed. The desk. Pointed my phone at the window. No luck.

Fine. I tossed the phone onto the mattress. There was a card on the desk with instructions for connecting to the lodge's wireless Internet. I could IM her on my computer . . . if only the connection had worked. I tried three times to log in, but I couldn't get a signal. There must have been a trick to it that I didn't know. Which meant that, for the time being, I was on my own.

Without my computer or phone, there was nothing for me to do in my room, but I wasn't about to go back downstairs. I wasn't ready to talk to Logan yet. I took my time unpacking, even though there wasn't much space to put anything. A lot of stuff I just left in the suitcase.

I did take out my decorations to personalize my room, even though my heart wasn't in it, in the hopes it would make my space less depressing. I tossed my Hello Kitty pillow on the bed, dropped my incense cone in its brass holder without lighting it, and *thunked* my grampa's picture on the dresser. I had just started hanging my string of twinkling lights around the room's tiny mirror when Mom knocked on the door and poked her head inside.

"Are you about done?" she asked. "Liz has some things she'd like to go over with us before dinner."

I left the lights dangling and followed Mom down the wide staircase to the main room. Liz was seated on one of the leather couches in front of the fireplace, with about a dozen gift bags arranged on the cushions to one side of her. Cavin sat on the other side. I stopped dead when I realized Logan was sitting opposite them on the other couch. I wanted to turn around and head back up to my room, but it was too late; Liz had already seen me.

"Very good," she said, powering up the tablet PC she held on her lap. "Everyone's here. Let's get started."

Mom dragged me to the couch, where she took the end seat, leaving me the cushion next to Logan. I sat stiffly, not really sure how I wanted to act around him. Or how he expected me to act. He said hi to me under his breath and I said hi back to him, but that was as far as it went.

"I've got some exciting developments to talk to you about," Liz gushed, oblivious. "Publicity has been working overtime, building on Cassidy's name recognition from her adventures in Spain and Greece."

She sounded so cheerful about it, as if all the half truths and made-up drama about me in the tabloids while I was there were good things. I looked to gauge my mom's reaction to Liz's chirpy attitude, but Mom appeared to be perfectly composed, her expression neutral. I tried to follow her example. One thing she always told me is that, as celebrities (although I still have a hard time thinking of myself as a celebrity), we are always "on." As I have learned all too well, you never know when someone could be watching (or worse, taking pictures). That philosophy has made my mom the queen of the unreadable face. I wasn't quite there yet.

"We've been able to line up some big-hitting sponsors for your shows," Liz continued, "and—"

"Wait. *Shows?*" I know I just said I was trying to act composed, but the last thing I'd heard, Logan and I were supposed to be doing little promotional spots for *When in Rome*. Thirty-second commercials, not shows.

"Oh, yes." Liz seemed delighted by my confusion. "That's one of the exciting developments I wanted to talk to you about. We ran Logan's head shots and audition tape past our teen focus group, and the response was overwhelmingly positive."

"You had head shots done?" I whispered to Logan. He didn't answer, but his cheeks might have gotten a little pinker.

"And Daniel was able to provide us some candid footage of the two of you in Spain. The chemistry between you is perfect."

Now I could feel my cheeks turn pink. It *was* perfect, wasn't it? Emphasis on "was." I didn't know if we had chemistry anymore. Not after Logan's comment about how fake I was on camera. And speaking of cameras, when exactly did Daniel film Logan and me together? Whatever footage he gave the network had to have been truly candid, because I thought Daniel was filming only when I was with Mateo; I didn't remember him pointing his camera at Logan and me alone. Then again, when I was with Logan and Mateo,

I wasn't really paying much attention to Daniel.

"We're so confident that the two of you will be a winning combination," Liz continued, "that we've decided to expand your on-air time. What we're looking at now is a running series of five-minute segments. Think Disney Channel's *As the Bell Rings*, only these shows will be unscripted."

"What does that mean, 'unscripted'?" Logan asked.

"Reality TV," Liz said gleefully. "We'll film the two of you throughout your stay in Costa Rica and edit the footage into four five-minute minisodes—mini episodes that will play throughout the week leading up to the *When in Rome* air date. With the two of you, it will be brilliant! Great idea to include Logan, Cassidy."

I flinched when she said that, hoping Logan didn't catch what she meant. But judging by the hard stare he gave me, he did. I should have told him earlier that the whole thing had been my idea, but he'd been upset about having to do the spots and I didn't want him to be mad at me. Now it was probably worse.

"Sorry," I mumbled. "I thought it would be fun to do this together." I might have said more, but he stared me down, so I pressed my lips together and looked straight ahead.

"Whoa, whoa, whoa." Liz's bubbly inflection melted away. "What's all this? We can't have any discord between the two of you; there's much too much riding on this project. So whatever little drama you've got going on, you need to resolve it this instant, understand?" She turned to Cavin and practically growled, "Tell me I didn't make a mistake investing in these kids."

"It's fine," Cavin assured her. "They simply haven't had the time ta settle in yet, is all."

Mom still looked as composed as ever, but the little muscle in her jaw was twitching, so I knew I was destined to have a "talk" with her once the meeting was over.

Liz regarded us for a moment, then launched back into her chipper routine. "Well, this might brighten things a bit. When we announced this project, sponsors literally lined up to support it. They've sent a few little things for you both to express their delight in working with you."

She turned to the assortment of gift bags and checked out a couple, rustling the tissue paper as she peered inside. "Ah, yes." She picked up a small blue bag. "Logan, this is for you. Your father said you enjoyed electronic games."

Logan hesitated for a second, then took the bag from her and dug in. "No way." When he looked up, his face had transformed, the scowl replaced by the biggest smile I'd seen from him in a long time. He pulled a brand-new Nintendo 3DS from his bag, along with a couple of boxed games. The top box was some kind of FIFA soccer game. It figured. When we were in Spain, Logan and our friend Mateo had completely shut me out when they talked football (or "footie," as Logan called it). Now he'd be able to tune me out whenever he wanted by playing a game. Perfect. "That version hasn't even been released yet," Liz told him proudly, and then she held out a large bag to me. "Cassidy, for you."

I rustled through the tissue to find a seriously adorable pink canvas Marc Jacobs cadet bag. I ran my fingers over the cool metal of the logo plate. Even though I didn't usually go for designer labels, I couldn't deny the bag was awesome.

"Open it up," Liz prodded. Then to my mom, "It's from the Marc spring line. Very hot item."

Inside were three different styles of Marc sunglasses, a cool Miss Marc scarf, different colors of flower earbuds, and several pairs of boxed earrings.

"They'd like Cassidy to wear some of their items during the shoots," she explained. "Down the line, we anticipate spreads in some of the teen magazines—'What Is *La Chica Moda* Wearing,' that sort of thing."

Mom's facade finally cracked. She shot a scathing look at Logan's dad. "Magazine spreads? Cavin?"

He cleared his throat. "Well, it's all speculation at this point. But the network feels, given Cassidy's marketing potential . . ." He let the words trail off because he didn't have to remind us of Lecture Number One. He was always talking about "striking while the iron was hot." It figured the network would want to milk my little burst of celebrity for all it was worth.

Now not only was the muscle in my mom's jaw full-on

twitching, but she had folded her arms tight and crossed her legs facing away from Cavin and Liz. Not good body language for discussing new ideas.

"Well, now." Despite Mom's attitude (or maybe because of it), Liz dialed up the perky about four notches. "Let's see what else we have in here, shall we?"

When she was done doling out the gift bags, I had enough earrings, scarves, and makeup to last me a year, a collection of designer sweaters and tanks, and a new military-style cargo jacket. Logan had scored a bunch of designer jeans and tees, a pair of cool sound-canceling headphones, and a FAI soccer jersey—signed by the team.

The final gift was the one that did me in, though. Liz handed Logan and me identical silver bags and practically bounced out of her seat waiting for us to open them. "They're matching smartphones!" she announced, as if we couldn't see for ourselves.

I glanced at Logan, wondering if he appreciated the irony of the timing. We'd never been able to text each other before because Logan didn't have a cell phone. Now that he did, and we could call and text anytime, we were hardly speaking.

If that thought crossed his mind, Logan sure didn't show it. He was too busy checking out the phone's features and messing around with the apps. I watched him sitting there in his new footie jersey, playing with his phone, and shook my head. Talk about being easily bought.

"Now then," Liz said, clapping her hands. "Are we all on board?"

Logan looked up from the phone. "Will I hafta act that I like something when I don't?"

"Oh, no." Liz shook her head, and the blunt line of her haircut quivered above her shoulders. "What we want are genuine reactions. You don't have to act at all. We'll edit out the negative."

"But that's not genuine, then, is it?" he asked. "If it's edited, I mean."

"I see what you're saying." She furrowed her brows, as if she was giving the question serious thought. "I tell you what. You can have final approval of the edited version before you do the voice-over, how's that?"

Logan put down the phone. "What kind of voice-over? I thought it was unscripted."

Liz's lips tightened around her smile until it looked like a grimace. "The *footage* will be unscripted," she said. "We'll craft a few lines after the final cut to introduce the episode, and to remind viewers to watch *When in Rome*." Before he could ask any more questions, she quickly turned to me and changed the subject.

"Cassidy, you'll want to add teasers to your blog. Give your fans a hint of what's coming. We can provide you with clips from the shoots to post if you'd like."

"Oh. Uh . . . thanks, but I sort of like to use my own video." I had always filmed my vlog entries by myself. As much as I liked the idea of including actual show clips, I didn't want to lose that kind of personal connection.

"Good idea," Liz agreed. "When you post them, be sure to mention that you took the videos with your new phone. The sponsors will love that." She made a note on her tablet and then turned to my mom. "If it's all right with you, we'd like to switch up the kids' shooting schedules a bit. While you're filming your longer segments, we thought perhaps we could hit some locations that will capture the younger demographic, such as zip-lining through the rain forest canopy, mountain biking, that sort of thing. Exactly *when* will depend largely upon the weather."

Mom said they would need to discuss supervision and security, but before they could do either, Liz declared the meeting was over. "Is anyone else starving?" she asked. "Who's ready for dinner?"

She and Cavin headed toward the dining room, my mom trailing close behind. "One more question, Liz," I heard Mom say before they disappeared around the corner.

And left me alone with Logan.

I sat awkwardly for a moment, feeling the weight of our earlier argument and trying to think of something to say. Not that he would have cared; when I turned to him, he had already loaded one of the game cartridges into his new game console and was thumbing the buttons, staring at the screen.

"I'm sorry," I said anyway.

Logan looked up at me like he hadn't even realized I was still there. "Huh?"

"I should have asked you before I talked to your dad about doing the spots with me."

"Okay," he said. And that was it. No apology for what he'd said earlier. Nothing. I toyed with the handle of one of the gift bags. He went back to his game.

"So . . . we're good?" I asked.

"Hmmm," he said.

Well. On the one hand, I was glad Logan had apparently accepted his fate as cohost, but I kind of expected that I'd say sorry and he'd say sorry and it would be like we were starting over. But where was my sorry? I pushed away from the couch and stalked out of the room.

Victoria met me in the doorway. "You forgot Man Fact Number One," she said. "Never try to talk to a guy when he's watching sports or playing a game. It never ends well."

Sure enough, Logan was still absorbed in his game. He hadn't even noticed I'd left him sitting there. "Guys can be so annoying," I grumbled.

Victoria laughed and slipped her arm around my shoulders, steering me into the dining room. "That," she said, "is Man Fact Number Two."

Travel tip: Costa Ricans are warm, friendly, and quick to smile. It is not uncommon for them to start a conversation, even with foreigners.

The table in the dining room was long enough that the entire cast and crew could sit together. That was something I really missed when I was shooting the travel special in Greece. I worked with a different crew there, and they hardly did anything together. They never came to feel like family to me the way our *When in Rome* crew did.

Logan managed to drag himself away from his game long enough to join us at the table. (Although I'm guessing that had something to do with his dad threatening to take the thing away from him if he didn't.)

Once we were all gathered, Cavin stood and pinged his spoon against his water glass. "May I have your attention, please!"

He waited for everyone around the table to quiet down, then held up his glass. "A toast," he said. "To us, to another successful show, and to our hostess, Señora Araya-Calderón." He gestured with his glass toward a smiling lady with short dark hair and a warm smile who was standing by the kitchen's swinging doors. She nodded back at him and gave the rest of us a small wave.

"*Sláinte!*" Cavin said.

Around the table, everyone repeated, "*Sláinte!*"

Britt whispered to Marco, "It's a traditional Irish toast. It means 'to your health.'"

Marco nodded his understanding and then he stood. "I would like to add a toast to welcome you to Costa Rica.

Here we say '*Pura vida.*' The words mean 'pure life,' but the better meaning says, Don't worry. Enjoy your life and be happy." He raised his glass. "*Pura vida!*"

We said it back to him. I liked the way the words moved in my mouth as they rolled out together: *poorah-veedah*. It felt comfortable and happy.

"And now," Cavin said, "let's dig in!"

Marco took his role as guide seriously, explaining to everyone what the dishes were as each one was passed around the table. It probably wasn't necessary, but I was glad he did. I've traveled with my parents enough that I've gotten pretty good about trying almost anything, but I still like to know what it is I'm putting in my mouth.

Our meal, Marco explained, was *comida típica*, typical Costa Rican food. The black beans and rice, for instance, would likely be served with most meals. There were also some corn pancakes called *chorreados*, a green bean and beef dish called *picadillo de vaincas*, and a bunch of other dishes whose names I forgot as soon as he said them. One of the most interesting was baked plantains with white cheese, because the flavor was so unexpected. Plantains look kind of like bananas, so I anticipated something sweet and smooth, but when I took a bite I was surprised to find the texture more like a potato. It might have been a little sweeter than a potato, but it was definitely not as sweet as a banana, especially with the cheese.

I snapped a quick picture of the plantains with my new phone to post on my blog.

When we were through eating, Señora Araya-Calderón started to clear the table, but Cavin asked the crew to stay where they were. They were going to review the itinerary for the next two weeks, he said. Since Logan and I were going to be on a different shoot schedule than the rest of the group, I figured I didn't need to stick around, so I grabbed a few of the empty dishes and cups and followed Señora Araya-Calderón into the kitchen.

"Muchas gracias," she said. "Thank you very much. But you are a guest. You should not work."

"It's okay." I set the dishes by the sink where she was rinsing out a pan. "I don't mind, *señora.*"

She clucked her tongue at me. "You must call me Mama Tica," she said. "I am your Costa Rican mama while you are here, eh? No need to say 'señora.'"

I couldn't help but smile. Her directness reminded me a lot of my gramma in Ohio. Señora Araya-Calderón didn't look anything like Gramma; she was much shorter—about half an inch shorter than me—and her black hair was only peppered with gray, while Gramma's was almost white, but her deep brown eyes—even though they looked completely different than Gramma's faded blue ones—held the same humor and warmth in them. I didn't know her at all, but being around her felt comfortable and familiar. "Mama Tica," I repeated.

"Yes. Very good. And you are Cassidy. I recognize you from your pictures. I am very happy to have you in my home, Cassidy."

"You live here, in the lodge?" I asked, surprised. I had thought the lodge was like a hotel or something.

"I live in the house up the hill with my husband and sons, but I think of the entire *finca* as my home." One more thing Señora Araya-Calderón—Mama Tica—had in common with Gramma.

I was about to tell her that when Victoria pushed through the swinging doors and into the kitchen. "There you are," she said to me. "I wondered where you went. Mama Tica, fabulous meal."

Victoria offered more help with the dishes, but Mama Tica chased us from the kitchen. "You girls go relax," she said. "The television says the rain will clear tomorrow, so you will have much to do before the clouds come again."

Victoria helped me to gather all my gift bags to carry them up to my room. Logan's had already been cleared away. He must have grabbed his stuff while I was in talking to Mama Tica. He was probably off playing his game again. A hollow feeling swelled in my chest. By now he and I should have been off somewhere together, talking, laughing, playing tricks on the crew.

"Would you like to go for a walk?" Victoria asked. "You look like you could use some fresh air, and Marco offered to show some of us around the farm before it gets dark."

Nothing against fresh air, Marco, or the farm, but a walk with the crew was the last thing I wanted just then. "That sounds cool," I said, "but I'm kind of tired. I'll probably just update my blog and go to bed early."

"Internet's down," Bayani said from the entry. "Apparently, the satellite connection goes out a lot with the rain."

Well, that explained why I wasn't able to get a signal earlier. And if the signal was still down, it also meant that I had no way to talk to Zoe. "Great," I muttered.

"I'm going into town to use one of the Internet cafés." Bayani pulled on his favorite Yankees varsity jacket, the truck keys jangling in his hand. "You can come along if you want."

I was about to say yes when I remembered I had just told Victoria I was tired. "Thanks, but—"

"Go on." Victoria nudged me forward. "Your public awaits."

In the time it took for our bumpy ride into town, the clouds had begun to lift, but ghostly trails of mist still drifted among the ferns and grasses along the sides of the road. I took pictures of the mist through my window as Bayani slid another one of his old classic rock CDs into the changer and cranked up Lynyrd Skynyrd on the stereo. He sang along to "Sweet Home Alabama," and I joined in with the chorus (it's the only part I know). Everything was going great until the song ended and the next song came on. "Free Bird." My stomach did a complete gainer. Last time I heard that song, Logan had been with me. Bayani had cranked up the music, and the three of us had air-guitared and head-banged all the way through.

If Bayani noticed my change in mood, he didn't say anything. He did turn the music down a little, though, as we got closer to town. "Help me keep a lookout," he told me. "Monteverde's a tourist town, so you know they've got to have a lot of Internet hangouts. Some places don't look like they would offer Internet service, but they do."

Sure enough, as we rounded a bend in the road, Bayani spotted a sign for an Internet café in—get this—a converted yellow school bus tucked back in the trees. "Oh, we gotta go here," Bayani said. "This is epic. And check out the name. Isn't that the thing Marco toasted at dinner?"

Along the entire length of the bus hung a bright blue banner that read, INTERNET CAFÉ AND LAUNDRY PURA VIDA The laundry part must have been in the little building behind the bus, I guessed. I snapped a couple of quick shots of it to post on my blog.

I read the sign aloud, feeling those words roll through my mouth again. *"Pura vida."*

"Pura vida," Bayani repeated. His *pura* sounded more like *purrrrrra*. Show-off. He knew I couldn't roll my *r*'s very well.

"Don't you have a word in the Philippines that means

the same kind of thing?" I asked as he parked the truck. "*'Mubahay'* or something?"

"That's not exactly the same," he said. "Sounds like this *'pura vida'* is more like that *Lion King* '*hakuna matata.'* You know, no worries, enjoy life, make the best of it. That sort of thing."

He turned off the engine and his regular smart-aleck grin disappeared. "It might not be the same word as we use, but it's something I can relate to. We didn't have much where I grew up, but we never let it beat us. Whatever you call it, you gotta live life, you know? You don't like it? You fix it. Just be happy . . . like me." He waggled his eyebrows, and the serious moment was gone.

I liked what he said, though. You don't like it, fix it. The thing with Logan was partially my fault. Okay, it was my fault. I shouldn't have volunteered him to do anything without asking him first. I didn't like what he said about the fake acting, but he probably didn't mean it personally. He's not like that.

By the time we walked up to the open door of the bus, I had convinced myself that everything was going to be fine. I could smooth things over with Logan. I could quit being so sensitive. As long as I was in Costa Rica, I could give the *pura vida* thing a shot.

But that was before I knew what was waiting for me when I signed in to my blog.

Travel tip: Costa Ricans have a deep

sense of honor, and care should be taken not to say anything that could in the slightest be interpreted as disrespectful.

The interior of the bus had been converted into a long, narrow room with a line of computer booths down one side and a few chairs and café tables down the other. Most of the booths were already taken, so Bayani went to sit at one of the empty spots near the exit end of the bus. I settled into a chair closer to where the driver's seat would have been.

The connection was pretty slow, but I supposed if Mama Tica's Internet was down because of the weather, it made sense that the rain could have affected the café's service as well. I tapped on the desk impatiently while I waited for the Pura Vida café home page to load. I had to repeat the process two more times to bring up my e-mail site and then to sign in to chat. After all that waiting, Zoe wasn't even online. Her icon sat there dark and unresponsive. Which made sense since it was, like, two in the morning in Greece, but that didn't stop me from being disappointed.

Down at the end of the row, Bayani was earnestly pecking away at his keyboard. From the look on his face as he watched the computer screen, we were going to be there for a while. I blew out a long breath. Well, I may was well update my blog, since that's what I said I was going to do in the first place.

I unenthusiastically signed out of chat and switched to the *When in Rome* website. It took forever to load. And *then* I had to sign into my blog and wait all over again for the main page to come up. One thing was for sure: at this rate, I'd never get a vlog posted. I'd die and fossilize before the connection would upload any photos, let alone a video. A short post would have to do. I could write something about my first impressions of Costa Rica. I composed the opening sentences in my head as I waited for the blog page to load. Maybe that's why it took me a moment to process what I saw on that page when it finally did.

My blog had already been updated, only not by me.

● ● ● ● ●

I first started keeping a blog because my grampa got sick. My posts were letters to him with pictures of all the places my mom and dad and I went for the show. Fans of *When in Rome* started to read my entries, and it didn't take the network long to notice the amount of traffic my blog was getting. As the number of followers grew, the network decided to move my blog onto their website so they could give me more bandwidth, updated features, and more security. Everything through the network site was fire-walled, encrypted, and password protected. So who could have accessed my account?

I didn't panic. Not yet. Mostly, I was just mad. At first, all I could think was that someone at the network had gotten impatient for me to update the blog. Now that they were using me to promote my mom and dad's show, they liked for me to post new content on the blog at least two or three times a week. It had been three days since my last post, but since I'd either been packing or traveling the entire time, you'd think they could cut me some slack.

The thing was, it didn't make sense that they'd get antsy over three days. I'd gone half a week between posts before, and no one at the network ever said anything, let alone stepped in to post for me. Besides, the network always stressed that we had to be respectful to our host countries, so if they ever did take over, this is not the kind of thing they would write:

Costa Rica sucks. Rain, mud, clouds, gloom. What
are these people thinking? Why do they stay here?
Why do I have to come here? I hate this place. I
hate the show. I hate my stuck-up partner. Can I go
home now? Yes, please.

I reread the bit about the partner, and an icy wave
crashed over me. It had to be talking about Logan. Who
outside of the network knew anyone was going to be filming shows with me?

"Um, Bayani?" I called weakly. "Can you come look
at this?"

He gave me a distracted wave without even looking up.
"Yeah," he said. "Just a minute."

I fidgeted with the leather cord of my charm necklace.
My grampa had given it to me for luck, and I could use
some luck now. Breathe, I told myself. Just breathe. Maybe
this thing wasn't as scary as I was making it out to be. I
mean, anyone could have heard about Logan working with
me, right? Liz said the network had test-marketed head
shots of him. They had lined up sponsors. That he was
going to be my partner was hardly a secret.

And once I thought about it, I was pretty sure I knew
who was behind the post. Tabloids have been known to
hack into people's private accounts. What would stop
them from messing with my blog? I'd had paparazzi
hounding me since Spain, and I wouldn't put anything

past them. In fact, one of them could be watching me at that very moment.

I leaned back in my chair and pretended to stretch my arms over my head so I could take a quick glance around the bus. You never knew who could be a paparazzo. It could be the guy in the baseball cap at the computer next to mine, or the lady with the bright red lipstick sitting at one of the café tables. Well, if they were waiting for a reaction (beyond me calling for Bayani, I mean), they weren't going to get one. Squaring my shoulders, I sat up straight and arranged my face in a neutral expression the way my mom did.

Which was pretty hard to manage when I knew exactly what she and my dad were going to do when they heard about my blog. They were going to freak. After the way the paparazzi had stalked me in Spain, it was a miracle they ever let me get back in front of a camera again. It took Cavin four weeks and a whole lot of talking to convince them to let me go to Greece. Paparazzi had followed me around there, too, but at least that time it wasn't because of anything *I'd* done. Still, Mom and Dad were overprotective. If they thought someone was harassing me again, they'd probably lock me in a tower somewhere and seal the door. I'd never get the chance to give the *pura vida* attitude a shot. I'd never get to fix things with Logan.

Unless they never found out . . .

I looked closer at the fake blog post. The time stamp

was from less than two hours ago, which meant that since there'd been no Internet service at the farm, there was no way my mom or dad could have seen it.

I stole a quick glance down at the other end of the bus. Bayani hadn't moved. He didn't have to know about the rogue post, either. No one had to know. Before I could change my mind, I quickly highlighted the entry and hit Delete. The computer hummed as the progress bar lit up on the screen. Five percent. Ten. Twelve. Fifteen. I worried the charms on my necklace and bounced my foot. Seriously. Could the computer be any slower? Thirty-five percent. Forty.

"Okay," Bayani said. He pushed back his chair, though he was still watching something on his screen.

Sixty percent. Sixty-seven. Seventy-five.

He stood up.

Eighty-two percent.

Come on!

Ninety percent.

Bayani started walking toward the front of the bus.

Ninety-five percent. I bit my lip. Hard. (I don't recommend doing that; it hurt.)

"What do you need?" Bayani asked.

The bar completed its count and the offending post disappeared.

"Never mind." I waved him off. "My blog page wasn't

loading, and I thought maybe there was something wrong with it. But it finally came up, so we're good."

He shrugged and went back to his seat. I quickly wrote a few lines about Finca Calderón to replace the blog post I had deleted.

And I hoped I was right about not telling.

The next morning, I woke to the sun slanting in through the narrow window at the end of my room. Mama Tica was right; the clouds had lifted. Now the Monteverde that had been hidden by the mist was on full display—the farms, the hills, the trees, the *green*. I could even see the Arenal Volcano all the way across the lake, a cone of green and brown against a rosy sky.

Closer to home, workers in coveralls and black rubber boots were already busily moving in and out of a barn nestled at the bottom of the hill. On that hill, more cows than I could count hung out in groups, grazing or basking in the sun. I pulled away from the window, worried that I must have slept in. Then I remembered. Days on a farm started early.

I took a quick shower, got dressed, and hurried downstairs to look for Logan. We may have started off wrong the day before, but he was my best friend. The whole ride back from the Internet café, all I could think of was telling him about the weird blog post. But he'd already gone up to his room by the time Bayani and I got back to the lodge. I couldn't text him because my phone still had no signal. I'd just have to grab him before breakfast.

I followed the smell of eggs and beans, fresh bread, and coffee into the dining room. No one else was there yet except for Mama Tica, who was setting the table and humming to herself. She glanced up as I walked in and gave me a crinkly smile. "Good morning! *¿Que pasa, calabaza?*"

"*Que* what?" I asked.

"*Que pasa,*" she said. "It means, 'How is it going?'"

"And the other part?"

"Ah, that." She folded a napkin and set it neatly on the table. "It is an endearment. It means 'pumpkin.'"

I couldn't help but laugh. My gramma used to call me her little punkin' when I was younger. Someday Mama Tica would have to come to Ohio. She and Gramma would probably get along great.

. . . And Gramma would be appalled if she knew I was standing there idle while Mama Tica did all the work. "What can I do to help?" I asked.

"*May* I do to help," Victoria corrected as she walked into the room.

I pulled what I'm sure wasn't a very attractive face. "Do you have to do that? It's seven in the morning. Lessons haven't started yet."

"That," she said, "was not a lesson. It was a reminder of something you should already know."

"To answer," Mama Tica cut in, "you may do nothing, *calabaza*. You are my guest."

"I know. It's just—"

"You are very sweet," she said, "but your breakfast is waiting. Please, sit."

"Oh. Uh . . ." I looked helplessly back to the staircase. Where was Logan?

"Your mum and dad are on their way," Victoria assured me. "Let's have a seat. We can wait for them before we tuck into the food."

Parents. Right. If that's who she thought I was waiting for, I wasn't about to correct her.

It was about that moment that Britt and Marco strolled into the dining room. Not simply at the same time, but *together*. Which probably wouldn't have captured my attention except for the way that Britt was smiling at Marco— like she was a pageant queen or something. I raised my brows and nudged Victoria, but she didn't react at all.

"Buenas dias," Marco said, tipping his head to Victoria and then to me.

I said good morning in return and tried not to be too obvious about watching how he pulled a chair out for Britt or the way she flushed as he helped her scoot it back in once she sat down.

She was seriously crushing on him, and he wasn't exactly indifferent to her, either. The smile he gave her might have been a little less lovesick, but it was enough to set off a little spark of jealousy. Would Logan ever look at me that way?

At the moment, I'd settle for him showing up for breakfast so I could talk to him.

While we were waiting, Victoria pelted Marco with questions about the weather, the farm, the cloud forest, and a bunch of other stuff I don't remember. That's probably because my attention kept snapping to the door every time someone came into the dining room. First Bayani, then Daniel, then Liz, but no Logan. Where was he?

"Cassidy?" Victoria nudged me. "Did you hear what Marco asked you?"

It wasn't easy, but I pulled my attention away from the door and back to the conversation at the table. But even then I have to admit I was only half listening.

Marco wanted to introduce me to a couple of the local crew members, Claudia and Estefan. They were freelancers from San Jose or something like that. I admit I didn't pay much attention to what he was saying. I was too busy running my future conversation with Logan through my head. Should I start by apologizing for the day before or just go straight into telling him about my blog? I already said I was sorry, after all. He was the one who hadn't—

"There they are," Victoria said. She pointed out the two *tico* crew members I had seen at dinner the night before, and pulled me to my feet as they came into the room. Claudia had long, black hair pulled into a no-nonsense braid. Estefan was tall, and kept raising his thick brows as people spoke so that he constantly looked surprised. Marco made the introductions, and we took our seats again.

Still no sign of Logan.

I was just about to go looking for him when my mom and dad walked into the dining room, and the expression on my mom's face stopped me cold. Or, I should say, the *un*expression. She had that neutral thing going on, which meant she wasn't happy about something. And since she was looking straight at me, I could only guess that the thing she wasn't happy about involved me.

My heart sank. The only thing I could think was that she knew about the hacker, although I didn't know how that was possible. I had deleted the post, but maybe not quick enough. Maybe the post had already been archived. Or maybe someone at the network had seen it and told Mom and Dad and—

"'Morning, Cassie-bug," Dad chirped. He sniffed the air like a bloodhound. "Smells delicious!"

Huh. Okay, clearly he didn't know anything or he wouldn't be so cheerful. For sure Mom would have told him if she knew about my account being hacked (or, more to the point, me not telling them about it), so if he didn't know anything, that meant she didn't know anything.

I leaned back in my chair and let out the tension with a long sigh. I had to stop being so paranoid. There was nothing to worry about. Right?

But just to be sure . . . I pulled out my phone to see if I could check on my blog. It wasn't picking up a wireless signal, which was weird—the rain had moved on, so there was nothing to interfere with the Internet now. At least I could get online with the 4G signal. It might be a little slower, but—

"Cassidy." Mom shook her head. "Not at the table."

I murmured an apology and tucked the phone away.

"Mornin', everyone," Cavin called from the doorway. All that waiting for him and Logan, and I didn't even notice when they walked in. "Forgive our late arrival," he said, glancing pointedly at Logan. "Someone had a hard time of it this mornin', tryin' to peel the mattress from his back."

Logan yawned and dropped into the nearest chair. His eyes were still heavy-lidded from sleep, and his hair was damp from the shower. It curled in dark tendrils just above his collar. I have to admit it was kind of adorable.

Wouldn't you know he chose that moment to look up at me? He caught me watching him and cocked his head to one side, as if to ask, What?

"Uh . . ." My face grew hot, and I could just imagine how red it was getting. I should have just looked away, but I was flustered, and when I'm flustered, I tend to babble. "So, are you ready for today?" I cringed as soon as the perky words left my mouth. They sounded as fake as . . . well, as fake as they were.

And he knew it. He grinned, obviously enjoying my

discomfort. "Naw," he said, "but it sounds like you're ready enough for the both of us."

I wanted to slug him, but he was sitting two chairs away from me, and I would have had to go through Victoria and Cavin to get to him. So I laughed instead. At least the tease was real. This was the Logan I knew, the Logan I had been expecting to find yesterday.

"Well," I said, spreading my napkin daintily in my lap, "someone's got to carry the show."

"Really," he drawled. "'Cause I'm pretty sure the market test projected me as the favorite with the fans."

"Fans? No one knows who you are!"

His smile grew wider. "Not yet."

"Right," Liz cut in, talking over us, "now that everyone's here, let's review today's schedule, shall we?"

Logan gave me one last smirk and then ducked back behind his dad so he couldn't see me give him one in return. Cheater.

Liz ignored us both and launched into a recitation of the day's events for both groups. Ours sounded like the most fun—while Mom and Dad were off talking eco-tourism in Santa Elena, Logan and I would be zip-lining through the canopy and riding mountain bikes. After lessons, of course.

There are strict regulations that spell out exactly what a production company is supposed to do with the young talent on their shows. (I love being called "the talent.")

Even when we were filming outside the United States, and even though Logan was Irish and not American, since the network headquarters was in New York, they expected us to follow U.S. regulations. Which meant three hours of schooling every day.

I know three hours doesn't sound like a lot when a regular school day is twice that long, but believe me, a compressed day does not equal half the work. We have no breaks between classes, no time off for lunch. It's just three hours of study, study, study, and that's on top of the time we're on camera.

Cavin and Liz and Bayani went on to discuss all the boring details of that camera time with my mom and dad, like permits and setup and angles and that kind of stuff. I was more focused on Mama Tica as she refilled platters of eggs, cheese, toast, fresh fruit, and black beans with rice.

I know that last thing doesn't sound like something you'd expect to eat for breakfast, but I've been to enough places to realize that any food you get in the morning tastes great if you're hungry enough. Heck, in Japan, I ate fish for breakfast. I liked black beans and rice better.

And so did Logan, apparently. All through the meal, I kept trying to get his attention, but he was too busy shoveling in the beans and rice to look up. I swear, you'd think he hadn't seen food for a week. All he had to do was pull himself away from it for a second so I could signal that I wanted to talk, but he never did. I was contemplating pelting him with a piece of toast when Cavin pushed back in his chair.

"Splendid meal," he said to Mama Tica. *"Muchas gracias, señora."*

Finally, Logan finished eating and stood at the same time as his dad. I jumped up to follow them when Mom took my arm and tucked it around her own. "Before you go off for your lessons," she said quietly, "I'd like to have a quick word with you."

My heart not only stopped, it backpedaled a few beats. Maybe she knew after all. I watched wistfully as Bayani pulled Logan off somewhere, taking my chance to talk along with him. Not that it mattered anymore. I was too late. My mom was going to kill me, so talking to Logan wasn't going to help anyway. I trudged behind her as she led me to the couches in front of the great room fireplace.

"What is it?" I managed to squeak.

She regarded me for a moment and then said, "Sit down."

I sank obediently onto the couch cushions, which was probably just as well because my legs were shaking too badly to stand. My brain shifted into overdrive, racing to come up with a good reason for not telling anyone about the hacker.

Mom sat next to me. "Filming for your show begins today," she said.

"Yeah?" I asked cautiously.

"I want you to remember a few things before you get started."

I nodded, hoping that she wouldn't see the relief that she wasn't talking about my blog show on my face.

"Since your show is a reality format," Mom said, "the cameras will be following you throughout your day. They'll film everything, watching for the right situations, the right shots. It takes a lot of footage to edit into each five-minute episode."

I nodded again. I hadn't seen an unscripted show filmed before, but I had seen the number of takes that went into my mom and dad's show. Don't even get me started on the amount of film we went through for that special I did in Greece.

"If at any time you feel uncomfortable," Mom continued, "or you need a private moment, just ask Liz to turn the cameras off, understand?"

"I will," I promised.

"You remember we've talked about being 'on' whenever you're out in the public eye? Well, with this kind of program, you are going to have to be 'on' at home as well."

"I'll remember."

She wasn't satisfied with the quick answer. "It will be easier at first. You'll be quite aware when you're being filmed. But the camera will *always* be there, Cassidy.

After a while, you get so used to it, it tends to blend into the background."

"Stealth camera," I joked.

"You make light of it now, but it will be a different story when you forget the camera and say or do something you'd rather not have immortalized on film."

Okay, so it didn't sound quite as much fun when she put it like that. "We have the final say in what they can use, though, right?"

She squeezed my hand. "Oh, absolutely. We would not have agreed to this otherwise. But you do need to be aware. Your dad and I won't be with you at all your shoots. We may be going in opposite directions these next several days. Victoria will be on hand to watch out for you, but—"

I tightened my fingers around hers. "Mom, relax. It's going to be fine."

Which proves how much I know.

I got my first taste of the stealth

camera during class time. We were about halfway through a math worksheet when Liz slipped into the sitting room that was serving as our classroom. Behind her came Daniel and Claudia, schlepping a big black camera on a rolling tripod and a boom mic. A boom mic is basically a microphone attached to the end of a long pole. The boom operator holds it over your head to pick up your voice. Real inconspicuous.

Claudia set up the camera and spent a few minutes loudly instructing Daniel how to hold the boom. It looked like Daniel had been recruited to our group for more than makeup—which wasn't unusual for *When in Rome*. Since we worked with a small crew, they often doubled up on their jobs. For example, Daniel had taken a turn as cameraman in Spain . . . but at least he knew how to do that. He'd obviously never been a boom operator before.

"Go ahead with your lesson," Liz said. "Just pretend we're not here."

With comic timing, Daniel chose that moment to drop the boom pole. It clattered to the floor and must have caused terrible feedback, because he squawked and ripped off his headset and let loose a string of some very bad words.

I ducked away from the camera to cover my smile, but Logan didn't bother to hide his. He laughed out loud until he must have noticed how horrified Daniel looked.

"Sorry, man," Logan said, scooping up the mic. "Really. Let me help you with that."

"Mm-hmmm." Liz made a note on her tablet and then waved her hand at us like she was casting a spell. "Carry on."

The rest of our class time, I tried to mix my mom's admonition to be "on" with Liz's admonition to pretend the camera wasn't there and went back to my worksheet. I couldn't imagine they'd want to tape our lesson for long anyway. Really. With everything there was to see outside the lodge in Costa Rica, why would they want to waste three hours on a boring class session?

And yet they were still filming when we finished with math and moved on to the research papers Victoria assigned Logan and me to write.

She set a tall stack of pamphlets down on the conference table in front of us. "Costa Rica is known for its biodiversity," she told us. "The variety of flora and fauna in Costa Rica's forests is so diverse that scientists haven't even been able to name everything yet, even though they have cataloged over two thousand species of plants, four hundred different species of birds, hundreds of mammals, and even five hundred types of butterflies."

I thumbed through the photos in the top pamphlet as she talked. It showed a variety of colorful lizards. The next pamphlet was full of birds.

"You will see firsthand a number of these plants and animals when we go into the cloud forest," Victoria continued. "So what I would like for you to do in the next hour and a half is to familiarize yourself with as many species as possible. You will be selecting one as the subject of a research paper that will be due by the end of the week."

Logan held up one of the pamphlets with a bewildered look on his face. "You want us to research with these?"

She cleared her throat and glanced almost guiltily at the camera. "Actually, yes. Only until we can get some sort of Internet connection reestablished."

I closed the pamphlet I'd been looking through. "It's still down?"

"I'm afraid so," Victoria said. "Mama Tica said she would have someone come take a look at the satellite this afternoon while we are out filming in the rain forest canopy, so you should be able to do some online research tomorrow. For the time being, I'd like you to take a look through these. The photos are really quite extraordinary."

Logan shrugged and picked up a pamphlet with a picture of a gigantic spider on the front. I started reading a short article about an animal called a coatimundi. The one in the picture stood rigid on its hind legs, peeking at the camera with a guilty look on its face. Or muzzle. Or whatever. The coatimundi looked like a cross between a badger and an aardvark, with a tail like a lemur. The article said it was related to the raccoon. Beyond that, I couldn't tell you a thing, because even though I read the article, I couldn't concentrate on the words.

All I could think about was my blog. I had assumed it would be something I could manage from the lodge. What if someone hacked into it again? How would I find out without Internet access?

I'd have to ask Bayani to take me back to the bus, but we wouldn't be able to do that until dinnertime because our whole day was already scheduled. Plus, now I had a film crew on my tail. That's all I would need—to find another rogue post while the camera was rolling.

I stared at the coatimundi, feeling as guilty as it looked. I should have just said something to my mom and dad the minute I saw my account had been messed with. It was bad enough I decided not to tell, but then I had covered it up by deleting it and writing a new post. Which meant that I would have to keep covering. Because if my mom and dad found out about it now, they'd come unglued for sure. The only question was, how was I going to sneak away from the camera long enough to do that?

Travel tip: In Costa Rica, weather and environment usually dictate fashion choices.

The difference between a rain forest and a cloud forest is that a cloud forest is usually shrouded in clouds. Where a rain forest is warm and humid, a cloud forest— on account of the clouds—is cool and moist. So when Liz said we would be zip-lining through the cloud forest, I had expected the entire forest to be, well, cloudy. The sun was shining as we suited up to follow our guide into the trees.

Since we were going to be up in the canopy, walking out over suspension bridges and zip-lining from platform to platform, we had to strap on safety harnesses with big metal clips so we could hook onto the lines. They didn't look complicated to put on, but I had trouble with mine and had to step in and out of it about three times. That wouldn't have bothered me, except the camera was rolling the entire time. Lovely.

As we waited for the tram to pick us up and carry us to the first platform, I pulled out my Windbreaker. Even though it wasn't cloudy, the air was damp and chilly. I was glad Mama Tica had talked me into bringing the Windbreaker to wear over my designer hoodie.

Liz wasn't thrilled about it, though. "The sponsors expect their product to be seen," she insisted. "Is that really the kind of outfit *la chica moda* would wear?"

I had to laugh, looking down at the way the harness bunched my pants up around the tops of my thighs and cinched my hoodie in at the waist. I was hardly a fashion icon, Windbreaker or not.

And let me tell you—I didn't care a thing about *la chica moda* when the wind started to whistle through the metal mesh of our tram car as we rode slowly up, up, up. It tossed my hair and snaked up my pant legs, raising goose bumps I could feel through my clothes.

Across from me, Daniel shivered and hugged his arms. I'm guessing his shivers didn't have much to do with the cold, though. He peered over the edge of the car and asked in a squeaky voice, "How high did you say this thing went?"

Victoria patted his shoulder. "Don't worry. It's perfectly safe. You're going to be fine."

"Yeah," Logan drawled. "We're probably only about fifty-five meters above the ground."

Daniel's grip on his seat relaxed a little. "Oh. That's not so ba—"

"What's that to you Americans?" Logan asked innocently. "A hundred and eighty feet?"

Daniel groaned and white-knuckled the seat again. Victoria pursed her lips and shot Logan a dark look. "Now, now," she said soothingly to Daniel. "Simply don't look down."

"But isn't that the point?" Logan persisted, "to look down at the—"

"Hey." I grabbed his arm. "Why don't you come sit by me?"

Across from us, Marco chuckled. "We should give him credit for trying to be brave," he said.

"I don't get it." I lowered my voice, but the wind carried it away so I had to lean closer to Logan and Marco to be heard. "Why did he come if it's going to make him miserable? We could have let him stay back at the farm, or go with the regular *When in Rome* crew. I'm sure Mom would rather have him with her to keep touching up her makeup than do it herself."

"It's a challenge," Marco said. "This morning he mentioned he was afraid of heights. I may have told him to meet his challenges head-on."

I looked over at Daniel again. His eyes were closed, and it looked like Victoria was leading him through some kind of breathing exercises. "What if he hyperventilates?"

Marco laughed. "He won't."

"But," Logan said, "if he's gonna be traumatized . . ."

"He will have faced his fear and be stronger for it. To experience life is to truly live."

"Like *pura vida*," I said.

"Exactly."

"What's with the pow-wow?" Liz asked, scooting closer to Marco.

"We were talking about the height of the tram ride," Marco said.

"Oh, yes." She nodded. "Amazing view, isn't it? Claudia's getting some fabulous shots. But we'd like to get some footage of Cassidy and Logan as we reach the platform up top, so if you wouldn't mind . . ."

"Oh. Of course." To Logan and me, Marco said, "If you will excuse me. It appears I am in the way." He moved off to sit by Daniel and Victoria.

Liz slid over to take his spot. "Now," she said, "I know we had some difficulties this morning with the boom setup, which we obviously can't deal with up here, so we're going to be using lavs for your sound from now on."

"Lavs?" Logan asked.

"Lavaliers," Liz explained, although that didn't help much. Not until she showed us a transmitter box wired to a small, clip-on microphone. I'd always heard them called lapel mics. "Usually, we would strap the transmitter around your waist to fit at the small of your back, but while you're on the zip line, we'll have to secure it in your clothing so it won't interfere with your harness."

Logan said it was cool, but I wasn't so sure. With a boom mic, you knew when your words were being recorded. That long pole hanging over your head was kind of a good reminder. With lavaliers, it would be easy to forget. We'd have to be careful about every word we said. I still hadn't had a chance to talk to Logan about the weird blog post—and I never would, as long as I was wired for sound.

When the tram stopped, Logan and I had to wait while everyone else cleared the car so that Claudia could get shots of us stepping out onto the platform for the first time. I didn't need a script to direct my reaction; my awe was completely genuine. It was like we had just entered some kind of fantasy world. The platform stood in the midst of the forest's canopy, and before us, a long open-air bridge stretched out into the treetops. Clouds I hadn't seen from below swirled around us so that the trees, the bridge, and everything below seemed to dissolve in the mist.

"It's so quiet up here," I whispered. The only sound I could hear were the buckles on our harnesses clanking as we moved, the gears on the tram lowering our car to the ground, and the very faint voices of another group somewhere in the distance.

Logan nudged me. "Check it out. There are *plants* growing on the branches of this tree."

"Those are called epiphytes," Victoria informed us. "They are plants that don't need soil to attach themselves to their host. You're probably familiar with some epiphytes such as mosses and vines, but"—she gestured for us to follow her to the bridge—"look how spectacular these air plants are."

From the suspension bridge, we were able to get a closer look at the trunk of another huge tree. The epiphytes growing there were spiky and flaming red.

"Have you ever seen such a color palette in nature?" Victoria asked in a reverent tone.

Once when *When in Rome* was filming in Curaçao, we got to go snorkeling near one of the most beautiful coral reefs I had ever seen. The variety and colors of the fish we saw were unbelievable. I never thought I'd be as awed by nature again, until now.

All around us, bright bursts of color dotted the mossy green background of the tree trunks—bromeliads, orchids, Technicolor birds. I took probably two dozen pictures of it all with my phone, but I knew that none of those pictures would live up to seeing it in person.

"Get that, would you?" Liz said, nudging Claudia. I thought she was talking about getting a shot of the scenery, so I stepped back out of the way.

"No, no!" Liz scolded. "That was perfect, you taking pictures with your sponsor-gifted phone. Do it again."

"Unscripted, huh?" Logan said under his breath.

"You want unscripted?" I pointed my phone's camera at him. He pulled a face just as I snapped the picture. I saved it on the screen. "Oh, very attractive. Your focus group will love this one."

"How about this?" He pulled his lips back and stuck out his tongue.

"Okay," Liz said. "That's enough. Let's move on, shall we?"

Marco quickly stepped into his guide role and led us across the bridge. The way that the clouds swirled around our feet once we moved away from the platform, it looked like the thing was suspended in midair. Daniel gripped the handrails and slid one foot in front of the other, mumbling to himself about not looking down. Which wouldn't have been that bad, to be honest, since all he'd see would be clouds.

Suddenly, Marco stopped and turned to face us. "You are standing," he said dramatically, "directly above the spine of the Continental Divide."

Ever the teacher, Victoria asked Logan and me if we knew what that meant. I had just read about it in one of the brochures she had given us that morning, and I was about to raise my hand with the answer when Logan spoke up.

"If I spit off the left side of the bridge," he said, "eventually it'll end up in the Pacific Ocean, and if I spit off the right, it will flow to the Caribbean Sea."

I smacked his arm. "Gross."

"Simplistic," Victoria said, "but you are correct. The flow of rivers and streams run west on one side of the divide and east on the other. Very good."

"I knew that," I muttered.

We ended our bridge tour at the platform for launching

the first of the zip lines. Daniel took up camera duty on the launching platform, and Claudia split from us to set up on the lower platform so she could film us as we arrived.

As we waited for her to get situated, the line workers gave Logan and me leather gloves to wear and instructed us on how to hold on to the harness and how we could slow ourselves by gripping the line if we needed to. They gave us funny-looking helmets with built-in cameras in them and helped us strap them on. It was hard to feel like any kind of a star while trussed up with the flat little helmet on my head, but as I stood at the edge of the platform waiting to launch, I didn't really care about that. I just prayed the ropes would hold, because in the mist, it looked like I was going to be jumping off into nothing.

When Claudia radioed that she was ready, Logan quickly volunteered to go first. The workers helped him clip onto the line, he gave a little wave to the camera Daniel was holding, and then he was gone.

"My," Victoria said, "that's fast."

I tried not to think about just *how* fast as the workers moved me into position. They fastened my clip onto the line, and we waited for the all clear so we'd know Logan had reached the next platform.

Before I knew it, the gate before me opened and I was off, flying solo through the trees. Above my head, the pulley hummed in a high pitch as it zipped along the line. Wind rushed in my ears. Those were the only sounds I heard. Even the chirping of the birds and the constant *thrum, thrum* of the insects was lost.

Logan was waiting for me at the bottom with a huge grin on his face. "That was awesome!" He pulled me into a quick hug as soon as I was released from the line. "Wasn't that wicked?"

"Amazing," I managed, even though my heart was racing and I could hardly breathe. Part of that was from the ride on the line, but a lot of it probably had to do with the hug and the fact that Logan's arm was still draped around my shoulders. I tried not to read too much into it—I knew Logan was caught up in the moment. Still, it made the moment that much better for me.

Daniel came down the line next, but I don't think he shared our enthusiasm. In fact, it looked like he was about to puke as the workers unstrapped him. He made his way shakily to the waiting bench to sit down.

"Eyes closed the whole time," he said, "but I did it!"

I wondered if that was the way *pura vida* worked. If you faced a challenge, you didn't let it stop you. You just closed your eyes and jumped.

Back at the lodge, the group split up as soon as we reached the front doors. Daniel excused himself for a well-deserved nap, Marco left for some quiet time, Victoria went to work on our lessons for the next day, and Liz had to take a phone call. That left Logan and me with Claudia, who went straight to work, setting up the camera on a tripod in the main room.

"Well," I said to Logan, "it looks like it's just you and me." I hoped that, in pointing it out, he'd get the hint and stick around. He did.

We sank down on one of the couches, but Claudia stiffly informed us that we had to sit on the *other* couch, so we'd be facing the camera. We obediently moved.

Logan pulled out his phone. "Have you seen the video camera on these things?" he asked. "Excellent zoom." He pointed it at Claudia, who gave him an exasperated look but otherwise showed no reaction at all. I pulled out my phone as well and we both filmed her, zooming in on the most unflattering angles we could find—the beginnings of a muffin top above her belt, a mole on her neck, the cowlick in her hair that made her bangs hang just a little bit funny.

"You know," Victoria said as she walked up behind us, "you could make more constructive use of your time. Start on your research paper. Read a book. Cassidy, you could update your blog."

She would have to remind me of that. Talk about bringing the good times to a screeching halt. Suddenly, all my worries about the weird blog entry from the day before came flooding back, and then some.

"Anyone know if the Wi-Fi's been fixed?" I asked. Claudia shrugged silently from behind the camera. Right.

She was recording us. Which meant I had to get away. At least until I could hide my anxiety better. The last thing I needed was for it to be preserved on video. I pushed off the couch. "I'll be right back," I said in a bubbly voice. "I'm going to go check to see if it's working."

"Don't bother." Logan held out his phone so I could see the screen. "No Wi-Fi bars. Must still be down."

"Oh. Uh." I kept working my way out of the shot. "I can ask Mama Tica about it. Where is she?"

"I believe Marco said she was taking care of the horses," Victoria said. "I'd be happy to walk down and—"

"No," I said quickly. "It's okay. I can go."

Logan started to get up. "I'll come with you."

"Good idea," Claudia said, "a walk to the stables would make for better footage than the interior of the lodge." She started to unscrew the camera from the tripod.

"No. Really. I'm just going to run over there. I'll be right back."

I spun around and dashed out the door before Claudia had time to protest. I just wished I had also managed to make my exit before I saw the confusion and hurt on Logan's face when I left him behind.

I found Mama Tica in the stable, hanging a bridle on one of the pegs that lined the rough wooden wall. I wrinkled my nose at the sweet-rotten barnyard smell of old hay and cow poop. Or—seeing as there were five horses but no cow in sight—horse poop. Whatever it was, there was a smelly brown pile of it near the empty first stall. Someone must have just mucked it out. Is it really weird that I suddenly missed doing the farm chores with my gramma?

The horse in the second stall heard me or sensed me standing there, because his ears flicked and he tossed his head the way Logan sometimes did when his hair got in his eyes. The horse nickered and shifted in his stall, and Mama Tica glanced up, a warm smile brightening her face. "*¿Que pasa, calabaza?*"

"Um, *pura vida*," I replied.

"Oh, very good. You answer like a *tica*."

"Claudia told me that's what to say," I admitted.

"I see." She picked up a brush from a cubicle and motioned for me to come in. "I am brushing Cholo. Would you like to join me?"

"Cholo?"

"This big boy." She patted the dappled gray next to her on the rump.

"Hey, I know him," I said. "He was out on the grass this morning. I thought he was lost."

"Lost? No, not Cholo. He's *el abuelo*—the grand-daddy—on this farm. He goes where he pleases."

Cholo apparently recognized his name because he whinnied and bobbed his head up and down, his hooves clopping on the stable floor as he danced in his stall.

Mama Tica laughed. "*Sí, sí, papí*. We are talking about you."

I carefully stepped around the pungent pile of whatever it was and took the soft-bristle brush Mama Tica held out for me. She was still working the stiffer dandy brush over Cholo's flanks. "You can start on his neck and shoulders," she told me. "I will finish getting the mud out back here."

The wooden oval handle fit snugly against my palm. I ran the bristles over Cholo's coat in gentle, long strokes. It felt like the most natural thing ever, even though it had been years since I'd groomed a horse. Mama Tica began to hum as we worked. I didn't recognize the tune, but it was happy, like Mama Tica.

After several minutes, I asked her for a currycomb to clean the hairs out of the brush bristles. She handed it to me, along with an approving smile. "You know your way around a horse, *calabaza*."

"A little," I admitted. Gramma and Grampa used to have horses on their farm, but they gave them up when Grampa retired. Only animals that earned their keep could stay, Gramma said. I remember how disappointed I was the next time we visited and I realized the horses were gone. It was stupid, really. Grampa and I used to ride the horses together, and I felt like they had given up something that belonged to *us*.

"What takes your thoughts so far away?" Mama Tica asked.

"Oh, nothing." I shook the memories from my head.

They were making me forget the whole reason why I had come to search for Mama Tica in the first place. "I was wondering if the Internet connection got fixed."

Her brows raised just a bit at the abrupt change of subject. "I am afraid not," she said. "Everything appears to be working as it should be, but there is no signal. I am sorry."

"It's okay," I said quickly. "Not a big deal."

Maybe I could convince Bayani to take me in to town when he got back. We could go back to that Internet bus. He probably wanted to check his e-mails or something. It might be tight, trying to slip away before mountain biking, but I didn't have much choice. I couldn't ask Victoria to take me, because she always paid too much attention to what I was doing. Daniel didn't have an international driver's license, Claudia would probably bring her camera along, and Marco had disappeared the moment we got back to the farm.

I must have been frowning as I figured all that out, because Mama Tica's smile faded and she looked as if she blamed herself for the Internet malfunction. "Really," I assured her. "It's not a big deal." Maybe if I kept saying that, I'd believe it was true.

"Took you long enough," Logan said. He was still sitting on the couch right where I'd left him, fiddling with his phone. He gave me a half smile as I dropped onto the cushion beside him, but the rest of his expression was guarded.

"Mama Tica likes to talk," I said with a shrug. I know what he was really saying: I could have taken him along. He was right, but then Claudia would have followed, and I couldn't talk to him with the camera in our faces and the lavs wired to pick up every word.

He turned back to his phone as if the conversation was already over for him. "What did you find out?" he asked, although his tone said he didn't really care.

I tried to ignore the sting of his indifference. He wouldn't be acting like this if I could just tell him what was going on. Which I would like to do, as soon as we could get away from the camera. "The connection is still offline," I told Logan. "They don't know what's wrong with it."

He barely lifted his eyes from his phone's display screen. "That's good, then, aye? If there's no signal, the suits can't expect you to write on your blog, so it works for you."

I flopped back against the couch cushions. "Not really."

Logan studied me for a moment, frowning. He tugged on his bottom lip like he sometimes did in class when he was trying to figure out a difficult math problem. I tried to give him meaningful looks—as much as I dared to in front of the camera anyway. Trust me, they said. Be patient. I don't know if the message got across, but his posture finally relaxed when he looked away.

After a moment, he held his phone toward me to show me an app flashing on the screen. "Look at this one." He leaned back so that his head rested on the cushions just inches from mine.

Suddenly, all thoughts of feelings and blogs and Internet connections poofed right into oblivion. All I cared about—all I could even think about—was Logan sitting next to me, his arm touching mine, his smile so close that if I turned my head just slightly, I might just be able to—

"Hey," Claudia's voice cut into the daydream. "What happened to the sound? Sit up, you two. I think you've disconnected your mics."

5

I didn't remember to think about my blog again until I woke with a start in the middle of the night, a weird twinge deep in my stomach. It's not unusual when we travel for me to wake up disoriented. It kind of comes with the territory. But this was more than the usual feeling of being lost. It was like that panic you get when you're afraid of getting caught doing something wrong. But I hadn't been doing anything but sleeping.

Outside, the rain pelted against the windows and snaked down the glass, casting eerie, squiggling shadows around my tiny cubicle of a room. I quickly switched on my string of lights to chase the shadows away.

Cheerful twinkles of red, yellow, green, and blue danced

across the walls, across my bed, and across my desk, where my computer sat, unused.

My computer.

My blog.

Oh, crud.

I had meant to corner Bayani to take me to the Internet café, but I got sidetracked.

It had been raining again by the time my mom and dad's group got back to the lodge, and Bayani let everyone off at the door the way he had done for me the first night. They rushed inside, laughing, dripping, stomping, and shaking water from their hair. When Bayani came in from parking the SUV, he got sucked into a discussion about the rain, and I didn't get the chance to pull him aside.

Then Marco suddenly reappeared, as if he hadn't taken off somewhere all afternoon. Britt immediately became his shadow, although he wasn't very focused on her at first. "I've been out making the arrangements for the mountain bikes," he told Bayani, "but we'll have to schedule that activity for another day."

Bayani pulled off one sodden shoe and dropped it with a thud to the floor. "You think?"

I don't think Marco caught Bayani's sarcasm because he said with a completely serious face, "The trails would be much too muddy. However, I was able to get clearance for a night hike at the reserve. If everyone has slickers and boots—"

"With the network's equipment?" Cavin peeled a dripping wet jacket sleeve from his arm. "I think not. Let's plan for another evening, shall we?"

Marco didn't say anything, but his lips pinched ever so slightly. He probably thought we were a bunch of wimps, hiding out from the rain.

Britt must have interpreted his reaction the same way, because she said quickly, "I'd love to go on the hike."

She was rewarded with an indulgent smile from Marco. Logan exchanged a quick look with me and rolled his eyes. I had to turn away so Britt and Marco wouldn't see me laugh.

I would have asked Bayani about going to the bus after the rain/hike discussion wound down, but by then, Liz had come up with an alternate idea for filming since we were going to be staying in for the evening. She signaled Logan and me to come over to where she stood with Mama Tica.

"I just had a brilliant idea," she announced. "Mama Tica was telling me how she was preparing a variety of soups for tonight's dinner, and I thought, Why not put the two of you to work helping out in the kitchen? What better way to introduce Costa Rican food to your audience?"

Mama Tica looked confused. "It is only soup."

"It's Costa Rican soup," Liz clarified. "It will be interesting."

Mama Tica looked to Logan and me apologetically.

"The soups have been simmering for some time now. There's not really much to do. . . ."

The way Mama Tica was hedging, it was a pretty good guess that Liz hadn't asked her first before deciding we would invade the kitchen.

"If you don't mind—" I began, but Liz cut me off.

"Of course she doesn't mind," she said. "You'll be helping. Many hands make light work!"

"Well, if we can really help . . ."

Mama Tica gave me a wan smile. "I'm sure I can find something for you to do."

Liz clapped her hands. "Perfect. I'll have Claudia and Estefan set up, and we can get started."

"She certainly is energetic," Mama Tica said, watching Liz cross the room.

"That's one word for her," Logan muttered.

Mama Tica's brows pinched. "I'm sorry?"

"I really like the idea," I said, diverting the subject, "of different soups for a night like tonight."

"I thought you would," Mama Tica said. "My family loves a soup night when it's rainy and cold out."

"Thank you," Logan said.

She gave him a puzzled look. "For what?"

"For treating us like family."

"Well, naturally." Her smile finally made a full appearance. "I am your Mama Tica, after all." She allowed Logan to walk ahead of us toward the kitchen, and as we followed, she pointed to his back and mouthed to me, Very sweet boy.

I flushed as if she had just paid me a compliment instead of Logan.

There was no question who was in charge of Mama Tica's kitchen. Before she would let Logan and me even consider approaching the food, she made us put on white chef aprons and scrub up like we were surgeons. The whole time she was being wired for her lav mic, Mama Tica lectured us about being careful around sharp knives and boiling pots. Finally, we were allowed near the cutting boards, but as Claudia and Estefan tried to film from different angles, Mama Tica kept shooing them back out of what she said was her work space. She probably would have kicked them out of the kitchen altogether if it weren't for the fact that they were in there in the first place only to film Logan and me.

"Here we have the three choices for tonight. I will put the finishing touches on the bean soup. Logan, you'll be in charge of the beef stew. And Cassidy, you will complete the *pozol*."

My pot held some kind of corn and vegetable soup. It looked complete to me, so I didn't know what Mama Tica wanted me to do.

"I will show you, of course," she said.

All I had to do was to chop up a little cilantro to stir

into my *pozol*, but Logan had to trim the ends off a bag full of green beans and cut them to the correct length for his stew. Mama Tica showed us both how to use the knives properly, with our fingers curled under so we wouldn't accidentally get cut. Logan handled his knife like a pro.

I have to admit I was pretty impressed by Logan's culinary skills. Besides being a master chopper, he knew his way around a spice rack, and he even volunteered to knead the dough for the thick cheese tortillas we were making to serve with the soup.

"Wow, such a chef," I told him. "I never would have guessed."

"Yeah, well, I had no choice, living with Da," he said. "It was either learn to cook or starve."

"Starve?" Mama Tica asked, catching only the end of our conversation. "Anyone starves around here, they only have themselves to blame."

For an instant, I felt like I could have been standing in my gramma's kitchen. "My gramma says the exact same thing," I told Mama Tica.

She smiled. "Your grandmother sounds like a wise woman."

"Yeah. She's a lot like y—"

"Wait. Cut. Stop," Claudia called.

I blinked out of my memories, startled. I'd almost forgotten Claudia and Estefan were there.

"Battery's getting low." Claudia pointed out the blinking red light on the front of the camera. "I need to switch it out. Can you hold that thought?"

By the time the camera battery was changed, there wasn't much more to film. We had finished the soups to Mama Tica's satisfaction and helped her carry the pots into the dining room, where we set them up on chafers.

"This will keep the soup hot," she told us, "so you may relax this evening and eat whenever you would like. I'll be back to clear it away later." She set out some bread with our cheese tortillas just as my mom wandered into the dining room.

"So this is what smells so delicious," she said. "What a treat! Mama Tica, you've outdone yourself again."

"I had help," Mama Tica demurred, nodding at Logan and me.

Mom hovered as Mama Tica untied her apron and bundled up in her rain slicker for the dash to her own house.

"Why don't you stay with us for a while?" Mom asked. "I hate to see you go out in this deluge."

"*No es nada*. It is nothing," Mama Tica said. "I like the rain. It brings people together." She winked at me, and then she was gone.

She was right; the rain pretty much confined the crew inside together. Since the satellite wasn't working, no one split off to hibernate in their rooms with their computers or TVs. We all hung out together instead, laughing, talking, playing games, sampling the soups. It felt like home.

Claudia hovered with her camera for a while, but we were finally able to convince her to put it away and join the rest of the group. I mean, really. There's only so much footage you can film of people sitting around doing nothing. Estefan helped us undo the lav mics. He set them on the mantel next to Claudia's camera, and we were free.

Logan didn't leave my side all night . . . even when I completely dominated him in killer Uno. Yes, I know I was the only one in the room anywhere close to his age, but I didn't get the sense that he was hanging out with me by default. He could have gone to talk sports with Bayani at any time, but he didn't. That made me think that maybe things between us could be getting back to normal.

And it had kept me from sparing a single thought for the blog.

But now that it was quiet, I remembered, and I couldn't get it out of my head. I opened my computer, but even before it booted up, I knew I wasn't going to be able to get online. If the Internet had been out all afternoon while skies were clear, it sure wouldn't be working in the rain. But I had to see for myself. I had to know.

Sure enough, there was no connection. I grabbed my phone on the off chance I could access the Web with it, but it wasn't showing any signal bars, either. I even climbed onto my bed and held the phone up high, angling it toward the window. Nothing.

I slumped back down onto the mattress. It's probably

fine, I told myself. That weird blog post was most likely a one-time deal, and I had fixed it. There was nothing to worry about.

Unfortunately, I wasn't very convincing.

When I couldn't make myself go back to sleep, I rolled off the bed and paced back and forth across the room like a restless tiger in a too-small enclosure. It took only about three steps to cover the distance. I always thought that expression about walls closing in was overdramatic, but that's exactly what it felt like: the room was getting smaller. If I didn't get out, I was going to be crushed. Without even bothering to grab my robe or slippers, I rushed out the door and into the dark and silent hallway.

It didn't feel much better out there. What I needed was space. Room to breathe. I felt my way along the wall until I reached the railing that surrounded the balcony and stairs. The gas fireplace in the great room was still lit, although the flames had been turned down low. Shadow and light leaped over the furniture. It jumped and stretched up the walls, alive and playful.

I sighed with relief and tiptoed down the stairs. About halfway down, I could feel the temperature drop just a hint. Heat really does rise. I almost went back to my room to grab my robe, but I figured it would be warm by the fireplace, so I just hugged my arms as I hurried down the rest of the stairs and padded across the room.

"Couldn't sleep, either, huh?" Logan sat up from where he had been lying on the couch.

I clutched at my chest, where my heart had just about jumped right through my nightshirt. "Logan!" I stage-whispered. "What are you doing down here?"

"Same as you, I s'pose," he said. "Too quiet in my room."

He scooted over to make room for me, and I hesitated for a moment before sitting on the couch next to him. Even though earlier the evening had ended up feeling pretty normal between us, the shorts I was wearing beneath my pajama shirt weren't long enough to cover much. I tugged at the hem of the shirt when I finally sat, then drew my knees up to my chest, stretching the fabric over my bare legs. There wasn't much I could do about my hair, and I turned my face away from Logan for a second so I could check my breath.

He tilted his head so that the light from the fire cast half his face in shadow. "You okay?"

"Yes," I said too quickly. "Why shouldn't I be?" My voice sounded defensive. And high-pitched, like a third grader's.

"Um, you're kind of fidgety," he observed.

"I didn't know you'd be down here."

"Sorry. I can leave." He moved like he was going to get up from the couch, and I grabbed his arm.

"No! I mean . . . you can stay if you want."

He settled back down on the couch, and we both stared into the fire for a moment. Now that we were finally alone, my mind stumbled over itself trying to come up with something clever to say. I had nothing.

"Whadya think'll happen with the agenda for tomorrow?" Logan asked finally.

I shrugged. Really? The shooting schedule wasn't exactly what I had hoped we would talk about. "I guess it depends on if it keeps raining or not," I told him. "Maybe we can go biking like we were supposed to do today."

"And if it doesn't stop?"

"Then we'll probably have to go to one of the indoor places with the *When in Rome* group."

"Wow," he said flatly. "Exciting."

"Beats tromping around in the rain."

"I don't know. This stuff they're filming is supposed to be real, right? Why *not* tromp around in the rain?" He grinned at me. "Nice word, by the way. Victoria's influence?"

"What? Tromp is a perfectly fine verb. Very onomatopoeia."

He laughed softly. "Victoria, for sure."

I bumped my arm against his. "I do have my own vocabulary, you know."

"Oh, yes," he said with mock seriousness. "And a very impressive one at that."

"Shut up."

He was quiet for a moment, then tilted his head at me again. "It's actually not so bad, y'know."

"My vocabulary? Of course it's not bad. I'll have you know I—"

"Naw. I meant doin' the show with you."

I studied his face in the firelight, looking for any sign of a tease. He held my gaze steadily. Sincerely. "Thanks," I said. "It's not torture doing it with you, either."

He chuckled and bumped his arm against mine this time. "You could'a told me it was your idea."

I nodded and looked away. That would have been the easiest thing, of course. But I figured Logan's dad would have mentioned it to him. And to tell the truth, even though Logan and I had been talking online steadily since I left the show, I was still a little shy about telling him how much I liked him. I was afraid if I told him I had requested working with him, I would have to tell him why, and I didn't know how he would take it. "Sorry about that," I said softly.

"It's all right."

The conversation kind of died after that, but that was okay. For the first time since we were back together, I didn't feel like I had to say something to fill the space between us. We both sat and watched the flames in comfortable silence.

Have you ever noticed how hypnotic fire can be? I hadn't forgotten about the blog again, but I was able to push it to the back of my brain . . . my mushy, drowsy, zoning-out brain. Before long, my eyelids began to feel heavy, and my head even heavier. I wrapped my arms around my legs and rested my head on my knees. And then—I don't even know how it happened—I found myself off center, listing just a bit to the left, toward Logan. I was leaning against him. He was leaning against me. His head came to rest against mine. And maybe because of how mushy, drowsy, and zoned out I was, it felt completely natural.

We were in a cocoon of warmth from the fire, from the silence, from each other. I wanted to close my eyes and let myself drift away right there. But then I saw the light.

No, not *that* light. The tiny red blinking light on the camera Claudia had left on the mantel. In fact, it was the blinking that caught my attention. Like in the kitchen that afternoon when the battery was getting low.

Which meant the camera was on.

I jerked away from Logan, suddenly very awake.

He blinked and rubbed his eyes. "What's the matter?"

I pointed to the camera. "What did she do, leave it going all night?" I whispered.

"Could'a been on a motion detector," he whispered back. I don't know why we were whispering, because neither one of us was wired for sound. But you never know how much the camera's mic will pick up on its own.

"We, um, haven't really been moving. What does that mean?"

"It means it's time to clear out."

Without another word, we left the couch behind and hurried up the stairs. On the landing, we paused, but only long enough to nod good night to each other. The silence was no longer comfortable. All the way back to my room

I imagined a hundred red eyes watching me from every corner.

I slipped inside the door and pulled it tight behind me. How many cameras were out there, lurking to record Logan and me on the sly? I crawled into bed and pulled the covers up to my chin, even though I knew I could never close my eyes or I'd see the camera's red, blinking light staring at me. And hear my mom's voice telling me to be careful.

She would flip if she suspected Liz was using hidden cameras to get the "unscripted" footage. So would my dad. They'd put an end to the show before it even began. Then I'd never get a chance to hang out with Logan again the way we just had downstairs.

I rolled onto my side and watched the raindrops making their snakelike tracks down my window. And I made a decision. I wouldn't tell them about the camera just like I hadn't told them about the blog. I could handle it. I'd talk to Liz myself. Spare them the aggravation. When you thought about it, I was doing them a favor.

So why did I feel so guilty?

The next morning, I didn't know which

was worse: the continuous staccato beat of the rain on
the roof or the persistent nagging in my head that I had
done something wrong. I showered and got dressed, but
I couldn't work up the nerve to leave my room for fear I'd
run into Mom or Dad. They'd take one look at me and
know something was up. I needed to work on my neutral
expression before I could go down to breakfast.

I was practicing in front of the mirror when my phone
buzzed on the nightstand. All efforts at perfecting a poker
face were forgotten as I dove for the phone. The connection
must have been fixed! I had my first text!

I admit to a tiny pang of disappointment that the

message was from Zoe and not from Logan, but at the same time, getting a text at all deserved a fist pump. Maybe now things would get back to normal.

Or not.

Because what I read in Zoe's message told me that normal was a long way off.

> Is everything OK? Your blog today is unhappy. I think Victoria was nice. What happen? Write back! I worry for you.

This was not good. The only blog post I'd written since coming to Costa Rica said nothing about Victoria. The one I erased hadn't said anything about her, either. That could mean only one thing: my blog had been hacked into again. And if Zoe saw the "unhappy" post all the way in Greece, chances were that other people saw it, too. Like the network. Or my mom and dad. In which case, I was dead.

I typed a quick reply to Zoe, assuring her that I was fine and that Victoria really was nice. I promised to write more as soon as I could, but when I touched the Send prompt on the screen, nothing happened. I tried again. Not a blip. Which was probably because the connection bars had disappeared.

"No!" I jumped around the room, waving the phone above my head as if I could find hidden signals hanging in the air. No such luck. The connection was gone. I tossed the phone on the bed and rushed to my computer, even though

I already knew what I would find. Sure enough, no Internet connection, either.

This was not good. I closed my computer and hurried downstairs. Poker face or not, I needed to find Bayani and convince him to take me to the Internet café so I could see what Zoe was talking about. And fix it before my mom and dad fixed me.

Bayani was already eating by the time I reached the dining room for breakfast. I slipped into the chair beside him and accepted the bowl of fruit salad he passed to me.

"Hey, Bayani," I started, "do you think you could—"

Dad chose that moment to wave at me from across the table. "Good morning, Cassie-bug." It sounded more like a question than a greeting the way he said it. His hand hovered over the empty space next to him as if it was wondering why the chair was still vacant.

My breath caught for an instant. Did he know about the hacked post? I couldn't tell. *"Buenas dias, Papá,"* I said, trying to sound casual. My voice came out all chirpy. I spread my napkin on my lap and took a deep breath to erase some of the perky from my voice. "Did you sleep well?"

Dad's eyebrows hunched together. "Yes," he said slowly. "I slept . . . well. You?"

Sure, if you didn't count the panic attack in the middle of the night, or being haunted by the mantelpiece camera's blinking red light. "Same," I lied.

"Me, too," Bayani informed us, totally eavesdropping. "I love the rain. Slept like a baby."

"Well, that's it, then." Mom slid into the seat next to Dad. "The forecast hasn't changed. Rain and more rain. Looks like we'll be doubling up today." She paused long enough to give me a distracted smile. "Morning, honey."

I managed to say good morning back without letting too much relief creep into my voice. (I hope.) If she'd heard anything bad about my blog, she would have led with that, not with an update on the weather. I might still have time to fix whatever it was Zoe saw.

"Where's the shoot today?" I asked, proudly keeping my tone neutral.

"The Monteverde Cheese Factory," she said.

I groaned. "Are you serious? We're going to go watch people make *cheese*?"

Not that I have anything against cheese. I actually like it quite a lot. But, really? What kid my age is going to sit through a reality show about making cheese curds? No matter how much Liz prodded us, there was no way Logan and I could make that look exciting.

Mom and Dad kept talking about the day's scheduled segments and what they would have to adjust to accommodate the change in plans. While they were busy talking, I quickly asked Bayani about going to the Internet café.

"Sure," he said. "Maybe we can go this afternoon after the shoot."

"I was thinking more like this morning."

He shoved a forkful of fried plantains into his mouth and talked around it. "Sorry. Far as I know, you have lessons until eleven, then it's time to go to the cheese factory."

"But—"

"Hey, I don't make the rules."

"It doesn't have to take long," I begged. "I just need to—"

Victoria chose that moment to show up. She stood behind me and laid a hand on my shoulder. "Are you about finished? Liz would like you to get wired before class. Claudia and Estefan are working on Logan right now."

Since it was clear Bayani wasn't going to help me, I followed Victoria over to where Claudia was waiting for me, lav mic in hand. I stood numbly as she clipped the mic to my shirt and adjusted the receiver along my back. All I could think about was my blog. There had to be some way to get to a connected computer so I could check on it. I just had to come up with a plan. And quick.

Logan gave me the answer without even realizing it.

"Do we have to work on those research papers again today?" he asked Victoria. "I already read everything in those pamphlets about spider monkeys, and there's not enough to fill half a page."

"I am sorry about that." Victoria sighed. "I had planned on the two of you doing some Internet research, but with the connection down—"

"What if we went to an Internet café to look stuff up?" I asked. "Bayani and I found this really cool one that's built into a converted bus, and—"

"I don't think so," Victoria said. "We need to be ready to leave for the factory at eleven, and I don't know how we could get to the café and back before then."

Estefan lowered the camera. "I know this place," he offered. "We pass Internet Pura Vida to get to the factory. Very close."

Victoria hesitated. "I see. So you think we could stop at the café first, on our way to the cheese factory?"

"*Sí.* If you like."

I could have cheered out loud, but I kept cool for the camera as Victoria considered the merits of the idea.

"Well, then," she said, "let's find Liz, shall we? She'll want to know our change in plans."

I quickly learned that getting permission to go to the café was only half the battle. Liz, whom I suspect was going stir crazy after having been shut in with the rain all night, decided to come with us. Then she turned the whole thing into a huge production, grabbing Claudia to man the camera while Estefan was driving, and Daniel to touch up our hair and makeup, which meant we had to borrow some old seven-passenger van from the farm so everyone could ride together. She even made me go back up to my room to change because I had chosen to put on my own shirt that morning rather than one that the sponsors had given me.

"Let's not forget who butters our bread," she told me.

"That's not even how the saying goes," I muttered to Victoria. She just smiled and nudged me toward the stairs.

Sometimes it's not a good thing that Logan knows me so well. He watched me as the van bumped over the rutted roads, and no matter how hard I tried not to let him know I noticed, I couldn't help sneaking quick peeks at him over and over again. Finally, he caught my eye and raised his eyebrows in question. He turned his back on Claudia and her camera and mouthed, What's up?

I shrugged and looked away. We couldn't talk with our lav mics on, and even if we could, what good would it do to tell Logan about the blog? It wasn't his problem. As long as he didn't know anything, he couldn't get into trouble.

It's a good thing Victoria was sitting in the front seat with Estefan, or she would have seen right through me. I couldn't tell her about the blog, either. Which was a problem, because unlike Bayani, Victoria would actually check to see what I was doing on the computer. I had no idea how I was going to check on my blog without her knowing, but I figured I'd come up with something when the time came.

● ● ● ● ●

The time came sooner than I thought. The *ticka, ticka, ticka* of the van's turn signal drew my attention to the front just in time to see Estefan pulling into the familiar Café Pura Vida parking lot. I took a deep breath and started to climb out of my seat, but Liz stopped me.

"You two wait here," she said, including Logan in her directive. "Claudia and I will go inside and speak to the owners."

I sank back down onto the worn vinyl seat. This could take a while. Whenever we did a public shoot like this, we had to get signed releases from everyone who might possibly show up on film. Then we had to test the site for optimum light and camera angles. No doubt Claudia would study the line of computers where Logan and I would need to work, and choose the best ones. Which meant the people who were on those computers would have to be kicked off (and compensated). It could take forever.

Meanwhile, in the van, Daniel made Logan and me sit in turn while he primped and sprayed and powdered us to his satisfaction. I hardly noticed what he was doing; I was too busy watching the seconds tick away on my phone's digital stopwatch. The longer it took for Claudia and Liz to get the waivers they needed, the less time I was going to have to get my blog straightened out.

"Cassidy," Daniel scolded, "stop biting your nails!"

I looked at the jagged edge of my thumbnail. "Oh,

sorry." I hadn't even realized I was gnawing on it. "Do you, um, have a nail file?"

"I do." Victoria dug one from her purse. I took it and watched out the window some more as I sawed at my thumbnail.

Logan, done with his makeup session, slid into the seat next to me. He yanked the wire from his lav mic out of the receiver and reached behind me to do the same to mine. "What's with you?" he asked in a low voice.

"Huh?" I pulled my gaze from the window.

He grabbed the file to stop it. "You're going to draw blood."

I looked down at my thumb. "Oh."

"What's going on?" he asked again.

I liked the feel of his warm hand on mine. I liked it a lot. And I liked the way he was looking at me, so concerned, so sincere. Which is why I felt bad about lying. "It's Zoe," I told him. "She said she needed to talk, but I can't text when nothing is working, so I wanted Bayani to bring me to this place so I could get online and IM her or something, but then Liz was like, Let's all go! And now I don't know how I'm going to message her with everyone hovering so I can't even let her know I'm here when she needs a—"

He held up his hand like a traffic cop. "Wait. Slow down. You cooked all this up just so you could send Zoe a message?"

I dropped my eyes to my lap and toyed with the nail file. "Yes," I said in a small voice.

"Why didn't you just tell me?" he asked. "I can distract them long enough for you to do your thing. Nothing to worry about. Just type fast."

I wished he was right about there being nothing to worry about, but I knew better. If my mom and dad and Cavin ever found out that someone had hacked into my blog—not once, but twice—and that I hadn't told them about it, heads were going to roll. I didn't want Logan's to be one of those heads. And it would be if they thought he had been running interference for me. But maybe, if he didn't know anything about the blog, he'd be in the clear. That's how the theory worked anyway.

When Liz signaled, Daniel and Estefan held umbrellas high above our heads as they ushered Logan and me from the van to the bus.

"They're staring," Logan half whispered. I tried not to smile at the way he spoke out of one side of his mouth without moving his lips on the other side.

"They'll lose interest," I assured him. "Bayani and I were in here the other day, and no one paid any attention to us." Of course, we didn't have an entourage with us that day, and there were no cameras. You add those little accessories, and people are bound to be curious.

Turns out I was wrong about the people in the bus losing interest. When we passed through the converted bus's accordion doors, the handful of customers and the guy in a staff shirt were carefully *not* watching us, but they were most definitely interested. I could almost *feel* their furtive glances as we took our place at the two vacant computer carrels. They were probably wondering who the heck we were.

I didn't know whether to say hi to them or to pretend not to notice the ripple of curiosity our being there had caused. It wasn't a question of what I thought was polite or cool; with the cameras rolling, I had to consider what would play better on television. Of course, the producers could edit anything to make it look like what they wanted, regardless of how it really was, but I would rather give them something they could work with so they could keep it real. Well, as real as a reality show can be.

I set my spiral notebook on the desktop and carefully laid the pen next to it, still debating whether to play the scholar or the socialite. And then I heard the whisper.

The words were Spanish, but I had heard them before: *Aqui esta.* There she is. *La chica moda.*

Great. Just what I needed. I guess it wasn't a big secret or anything, but the extra attention kind of spoiled the plan to stealth-check my blog.

I logged onto the computer anyway, staring at the screen

as it loaded in an attempt to shut everything else out. It didn't work. I was hyper-aware of the whispering around me, of the camera at the end of the row pointed straight at me, and of Victoria standing patiently nearby to oversee Logan's and my research. This was going to be even harder than I thought.

True to his word, Logan distracted Victoria, asking for help to look up his monkey facts—as if he'd never googled anything before. For someone who just two days earlier had been complaining about having to be fake, he sure was good at putting on an act.

I waited until she was actually bending over his keyboard, helping him type in the words for his search, and then switched screens on my computer to look up my blog. Just as it had been the last time I was there, the computer was maddeningly slow. I switched screens back to my report search while the network page loaded. After writing down a random fact or two, I checked back to see if the prompt screen for my blog was ready. Another quick peek at Victoria, who was trying to be patient as she explained to Logan how to navigate an encyclopedia page with links, and I quickly signed into my blog. Switching screens once again, I waited, chewing on my overfiled thumbnail again.

When I switched back to my blog screen, I shouldn't have been surprised to see the entry there, but I was. Not exactly because there was an entry, but because of how long it was. The whole post couldn't even fit on the screen; I had to scroll down to see it all. Apparently, whoever was messing with my blog had a lot to say.

I skimmed through the post, and my eyes got wider and wider as I read.

"Monteverde is way boring. There's nothing but mud and potholes and losers swinging in the trees like monkeys."

My breath caught at the words "swinging in the trees." That sounded like it could be referring to the zip lines from the day before, right? If I didn't know better, I would have thought that whoever wrote that entry knew me as more than just some face in a tabloid. They knew what I was doing. Suddenly, the back of my neck went cold. I felt like a huge bull's-eye had been painted between my shoulder blades.

Turning slowly, I snuck a peek directly behind me. Of course there was no one there. But there were two guys by the old driver's seat staring at me. And a lady watching from the end carrel. And a man at one of the tables, who glanced up from his magazine just in time for his dark eyes to meet mine. Any one of them could be a paparazzo. Or all of them. Or none of them. How could anyone have known I was going to stop by the Internet café this morning? I was being paranoid. Or not. I read on.

My tutor is a Gorgon, always watching, waiting for
me to trip up so she can pounce on me and rip me
to shreds.

Why would someone write that? A chill, colder than
the rain outside, swept over me. My hacker wasn't just some
random person having fun showing what a computer genius
he or she was. These posts were mean. They were personal.

The question was, what was I going to do about it? I
chewed on my thumbnail some more (sorry, Daniel) and
stared at the screen. The first thing, of course, was to delete
the entry. Which, with the horrible Internet connection, was
going to take a while. I initiated the delete, and switched
screens as the computer slowly executed the command.

Even as the post dissolved, my stomach twisted into
sailor knots. I knew exactly what my mom and dad would
do if they saw that post; they would completely freak. And
then I wouldn't be able to continue doing the shows with
Logan, because my parents would probably lock me away in
protective custody somewhere. I was dead.

I'd deleted the post, sure, and the one before it. But
Mom always says what goes online stays online. You can
never tell if something has been copied or cached, so even
if you remove it, you can never be sure that a thing is truly
gone.

Given those facts, it would have been smart for me to
come clean, but I figured I was already in too deep. The

problem was, by keeping the secret, I was about to get deeper. I may have been a little distracted as we drove to the cheese factory. Victoria asked me three times if I was feeling "quite all right." Claudia had to tell me twice to fix the mic on my lapel because it kept coming loose. Even Logan noticed that I wasn't acting like myself.

"Did you . . . take care of what you needed to?" he asked.

I pulled at my newly adjusted lapel mic, wishing I could take the thing off and talk to him. I mean, really talk to him. About the blog. About what was going on. I knew without question he would understand what my mom and dad couldn't. Maybe he could even help me figure out what to do.

Not that I deserved his help. I hadn't exactly been honest with him when we went to the Internet café. "About that," I began. "It wasn't Zoe I was—"

"Oh, look at that," Victoria cut in. She pointed out the window to where an old wooden oxcart with brightly painted wheels rolled and swayed at the side of the road. Two gigantic black oxen with wide, curved horns plodded along pulling the cart, guided by a man in gray coveralls and black rubber boots. In the back of the cart, a half dozen shiny silver cylinders clanked against each other.

"*Esta leche*," Estefan called from the driver's seat. "The milk. This farmer is delivering to the cheese factory."

"Logan," I said, "about the café . . ."

Liz nudged Claudia and pointed out the window. "Get a shot of that."

"Way ahead of you." Claudia adjusted the angle of her camera to capture the farmer and his wagon of milk.

Usually, I would pull out my phone to take pictures for my blog as well, but I didn't touch it. Just thinking about the blog did unpleasant things to my stomach.

"Logan . . ."

"Please tell me the poor man lives nearby." Daniel tsked. "Imagine making your deliveries on foot."

"The cheese factory milk is local," Estefan said. "I do not know if this means nearby."

I tugged on Logan's sleeve. "Hey, I need to tell—"

Logan gave me one of those just-a-minute looks and talked to Estefan's image in the rearview mirror. "So all the local farmers drive carts like that? With the painted wheels?"

"*¿Las carretas?*" Estefan asked. "No, not many. From the small farm, perhaps, but many drive the truck."

"And everyone in the area sells to the factory?" Logan asked.

Estefan nodded. "Most do."

"Ah, yes," Victoria chimed in. "Mama Tica mentioned that Finca Calderón delivers their milk to the factory as well."

"That's a lot of milk," Logan said. "How much cheese do these guys make?"

"Oh, quite a lot," Victoria said. "They export it all over Central America. And other dairy products as well."

I shook my head and checked out of the conversation. Any other time, you couldn't pay Logan to sit still for a conversation about milk deliveries and painted carts, but now, when I needed to talk to him, he was the one keeping the stupid thing going.

Ironic, I thought sourly.

And the worst part was, I probably deserved it.

Six or seven people—civilians, Liz called them—were already gathered in the factory lobby when we got there, waiting for the tour to begin. They huddled together, whispering and trying not to stare as Daniel herded Logan and me into a corner to be powdered and sprayed some more while Estefan and Claudia walked around the room taking readings with their light meter. Then the regular *When in Rome* group arrived and pretty much took over the lobby. The civilians went from a group of curious onlookers to outright gawkers as Bayani and Britt helped Claudia and Estefan set up the cameras and sound equipment to follow the tour. Liz and Cavin strolled around the room with a representative of the factory, gesturing and pointing and talking (in not very soft voices, I might add) about where they would like to set up shots.

"Kinda creepy being watched like that," Logan whispered.

My breath caught for an instant until I realized he was talking about our civilian audience and not the faceless hacker I now suspected was spying on me.

Daniel stopped brushing my hair and pushed down on my shoulders. "Quit hunching. You want your posture to stay that way?"

I laughed—mostly to make myself relax. "What are you saying? Shoulders stick? Like crossed eyes?" My gramma hated it if I went cross-eyed. She swore one day my eyes would get stuck turning inward.

"Crossed eyes are nothing," Logan said. "Check this out." He folded his eyelids up so that they looked like they were turned inside out.

"Ew!" I turned away. "That's so gross!"

"You like that?" he teased. "Then you should see—"

"Logan! Cassidy!" Liz hissed. "Remember yourselves. You never know who could be watching."

Despite Daniel, my shoulders hitched up again. I hugged my arms and slid a quick glance around the lobby. That was exactly what I was afraid of.

I can't say that I remember much of the cheese factory tour. Not that it wasn't cool to see how eco-friendly the Quakers who established the factory were, right down to the wastewater disposal, but my mind wasn't with the tour. It was stuck on whoever was hacking my blog posts, and what I was going to do to stop it.

I had changed my password, but that was going to accomplish only so much. This person had gotten past the password—plus all the network's firewalls—once; he or she could do it again. Maybe I should talk to Britt. Of anyone on the crew, she was the expert on computers and security and that kind of thing. She'd know what to do.

But I didn't know Britt. If I confided in her, would she tell Mom and Dad? They would circle the wagons for sure. I had to test Britt out somehow. Maybe if I—

"Cassidy!" Liz's voice slammed into my thoughts. "This is supposed to be interesting. You look as if you're comatose. Could you liven it up a bit?"

"Yeah," Logan agreed. "You're not very gouda at this acting thing."

It took me a full ten seconds to realize what he had said. I laughed and shot back, "You cheddar stop being mean to me."

"What? You a feta a little humor?"

"Not if it's funny, you muenster!"

"Ha-ha." Liz said drily. "Now be serious. But don't forget to make it interesting."

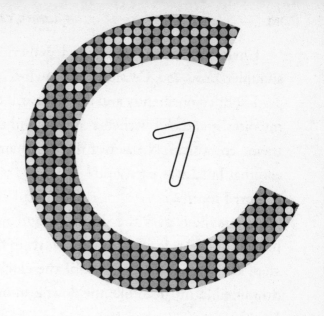

Travel tip: In Costa Rica, criticism is rare.

People would rather solve problems *"à la tica,"* bargaining to avoid conflict.

I never did get a chance to talk to Britt or anyone else about my blog because the network beat me to it. They called Liz early the next morning. I knew I was in trouble when Cavin blocked my mom and dad and me on our way down the stairs for breakfast.

"A word, please," he said, and gestured for us to follow him. Mom and Dad looked at each other with a mutual shrug and fell into step behind Cavin. I stood on the bottom stair and wished I could freeze time long enough to think of some way to disappear.

Cavin paused and shot me a withering look over his shoulder. "You, too, Cassidy," he growled.

I nodded obediently and forced myself to follow behind my mom and dad. I wished I could pull them aside to warn them. To explain. Neither of them had any clue what was coming, but I was pretty sure I did, and it wasn't going to play well for me.

We walked past the dining room in a slow-motion procession. At least that's how it felt to me. Every step, every breath, every tick of the clock in the hallway drummed in my head like the downbeat of a funeral dirge. I was so dead.

Logan was sitting at the table with Bayani, and he glanced up just in time to catch my eye before I passed the doorway. I looked away before he could read the mix of guilt and fear on my face.

Cavin held the door to the sitting room for us to file inside. I wasn't surprised to find Liz pacing on the other side of the conference table, where a single file folder lay close to the edge. She stopped when she saw us and drew herself up, puffing out her chest and planting her hands on her hips. She was doing a perfect imitation of a cobra, making herself look bigger and more intimidating. Was that a defensive gesture or a warning that she was about to strike?

"Please," she said in a calm-but-strained voice, "have a seat."

Mom and Dad exchanged one of those looks again and each sat down stiffly—just now realizing, I think, that this meeting wasn't going to be pleasant. I preferred to remain standing. If Liz was a snake, I'd be more prepared for flight by staying on my feet.

But then Cavin pulled out a chair for me and ordered me to sit. What else could I do but obey? I folded myself onto the chair, where I felt vulnerable and small. Especially when my mom and dad threw questioning looks at me and I could see the understanding light their faces as they realized we were meeting because of something I'd done.

Liz didn't even try to be pleasant or ease into the conversation. She planted both hands on the table and leaned forward like she was going to lunge at us. Without thinking, I sank farther back into my chair. "Who," Liz asked, "do you think called me early this morning?"

My mom and dad looked to me expectantly.

I mumbled that I didn't know.

"The network, Cassidy. Now why do you suppose they woke me up at five in the morning with a phone call?"

"Tone," Cavin reminded her.

She drew back from the table and took a deep breath before trying again in a sticky-sweet voice. "I'm sorry, Cassidy. Can you think of any reason why the network would be calling me?"

I would have liked to divert the question, but what good

would it do? Even though I didn't like the way Liz was talking to me, I knew why she was angry, so it wouldn't do any good to pretend I didn't. "They saw my blog," I said matter-of-factly.

"Your blog?" Mom shook her head. "I don't understand."

"Someone hacked into my blog," I told her in a small voice.

Dad turned to Cavin. "Someone hacked into her blog? Who? How did they get past the firewalls?"

"And how would that be Cassidy's fault?" my mom chimed in.

"It's not the hacking I'm concerned about," Liz said. "It's the hiding."

Mom and Dad looked back to me. "Hiding?" Dad asked.

I twisted the leather cord of my necklace around my fingers and shifted in my chair. "I wasn't really *hiding* anything. Some hacker posted a couple of rude things on my blog, and I deleted them."

"But not until a good number of people saw them," Liz said.

"Security of the website is not Cassidy's responsibility," Dad said. "You can hardly expect her to—"

"The first post appeared and was deleted two days ago," Liz told him.

Mom was the first one to make the connection. "You knew someone had hacked into your account two days ago and you didn't tell us?"

"I didn't want you to . . . worry about it." I almost said "overreact," but I stopped myself just in time.

"What sort of things did these hacked posts say?" Dad asked, but he didn't direct his question to me.

Liz picked up the file folder from the table and pulled a paper from it. She handed it to Dad. "These are the ones circulating at the moment."

"Circulating?" Mom was starting to sound like a parrot, the way she kept repeating everything.

"They're being Facebooked, tweeted, blogged about, you name it," Cavin said. "After the last vlog episode . . ."

I groaned. Did we really have to go there? When I was in Spain, a video I had posted on my blog went viral and caused a lot of drama. I would rather avoid a repeat in Costa Rica. "They were just short notes," I tried.

"Allow me to read you one of those *notes*," Liz said imperiously. She picked up the paper and snapped it straight in her hand. 'The town of Monteverde is nothing but mud and potholes and losers swinging in the trees like monkeys.' Or how about this one? 'This misery is compounded by the screaming stupidity of our director.'"

Dad winced. "This is circulating online?"

"According to Jack Angelos," Liz sniffed, "the catch-phrase 'screaming stupidity' has become a meme."

"And guess who picked it up on his blog?" Cavin asked. "Bryant Howell, our esteemed rival with *A Foreign Affair.*

He is 'appalled by the lack of respect' for our host country and for each other."

"But everyone knows I didn't write any of that, right?" I asked. "I mean, come on. That doesn't even sound real."

"It doesn't have to be real to take on a life of its own," Liz said. "The masses love a scandal—even if they have to make one up."

Mom had gone quiet, but the way she was sitting with her back rigid and her hands folded tightly in her lap, it was clear she was going to have plenty to say.

"How's it affecting the ratings?" I asked Cavin. Ratings were the only thing I could think of that would spin this mess in a positive light. When that other vlog post went viral, the network was actually thrilled because it made the ratings, as Cavin put it, go through the roof. Maybe this would do the same.

Mom looked at me darkly. "Our ratings are not the issue, Cassidy. You should have told us the moment you saw your account had been hacked. Not only to keep the situation from getting out of hand, but to keep you safe."

"I know." I twisted my necklace again. A parade of excuses waited to be spoken. I thought it was only a one-time thing. I thought when I deleted that first message, everything would be okay. I didn't have the Internet access to see that it wasn't. But excuses weren't going to cut it. Especially when I did know better. I hung my head. "I'm sorry."

"*When in Rome* has had an uptick," Liz said, and I looked up hopefully. That was a good thing, right? "But that does not translate into favorable prepublicity for the children's network. In fact," she leaned forward on the table again, "some of your biggest sponsors are threatening to pull out. They view this kind of thing as a lack of control. They don't wish to be associated with lack of control."

"Can we convince them to stay?" I asked in a small voice.

"We had better hope so," Liz said, "because without sponsors, we lose funding, and without funding, we're done."

I slumped in my chair as Cavin discussed the security changes they were putting in place to make sure my account didn't get hacked into again. New passwords, new firewalls, new accessibility. From now on, I couldn't post straight to my blog. I'd have to send all entries to a handler at the network who would approve the content and have it uploaded. Piece by piece, I had lost control over my own blog. Pretty soon they'd be writing it for me, too.

"Right," Cavin said when he wound down. "We'd better go grab some breakfast before it's cleared away. Our team has a full day ahead of us today."

Their team, meaning the *When in Rome* crew. "What about us?" I asked. "Will we keep filming?"

Liz straightened the face of the watch she wore on her wrist, looking past me rather than at me. "For now," she said. "Beyond that, we will see."

We filed out of the room in glum silence. I told my

mom and dad I wasn't hungry for breakfast, but really, I didn't want to sit with everyone else at the table and try to pretend everything was okay. Plus, Liz said we'd keep filming for now, and if either Claudia or Estefan was waiting in the dining room with a camera, that's the last place I wanted to be.

I started for the stairs when I noticed Logan sitting in the wingback chair I'd seen him in that first night. "Did you already eat?" I asked.

He ignored my question. "What was it you didn't want anyone to see you looking at yesterday at that Internet place?"

I sank onto the ottoman. Oh, great. He knew, too. "My blog. I wanted to make sure it hadn't been hacked into again." It had, but I didn't think adding that little detail would help.

"You didn't think you could tell me what was up?"

I sighed, too weary to go over everything again. Yes, I should have told him. Yes, I was wrong. What did he want me to say?

"You can trust me," he persisted. "Don't you know that by now?"

"No, not really," I shot back. "You haven't exactly been yourself this trip. It's hard to know what to expect with you."

His jaw tightened and he shook his head, then nodded, then shook his head again. "Well, excuse me," he said evenly, "but it's a wee bit difficult to be yourself with a camera in your face all day."

I laughed. "Welcome to my world, Logan." It came out sounding harsher than I intended, so I took a deep breath and tried again. "I didn't want you to get into trouble if you knew," I said. "I was trying to protect you."

He stood, looking down on me with a mixture of disappointment and sadness. "I don't want to be protected," he said. "I want to be trusted."

I wanted to yell after him as he walked away, but (a) I didn't know what I would say, and (b) everyone else in the house would hear it, too. For the first time, I wished Mom and Dad had accepted the rooms in the casita. At least then I could scream in private.

I pushed off the ottoman and paced, so full of frustrated energy I thought I would burst. Who else was going to lay into me that morning? Bayani? He could tell me how wounded he was that I got him to take me to the Internet bus that first night. Or Victoria? She could tell me she was scarred for life because I didn't want her to see me checking the blog. Who else? They might as well all come forward now while Dump on Cassidy Day was in progress.

In the dining room, it looked like everyone had split into groups. Cavin, Liz, and my mom and dad sat at one end; Victoria, Bayani, and Daniel huddled at the other. Claudia and Estefan sat talking in the middle and looked

up in time to see me standing, watching. Claudia frowned
and said something to Estefan, who nodded in agreement.

I didn't stick around to find out what she said. I couldn't.
I had to get away from the house. Away from everyone *in*
the house.

I slipped out the front door and leaned my back against
it, blinking back tears. I wanted to run off the energy, but
the ground was soggy—not so great for running—so I
walked instead. I didn't even realize where I was going until
I almost reached the stable.

Mama Tica was settling a worn leather saddle onto one
of the horses, and she glanced up when I reached the door.
"Hey! *¿Que pasa, calabaza?*"

"*Pura vida,*" I mumbled.

"Well, now. That did not sound very convincing. Could
you help me for a moment?" She motioned for me to come
closer. "Just hold this if you would."

She handed me the lead and then bent down to cinch
the saddle. "Talk to her softly," she said. "Paca likes that."

"Paca," I repeated. "That's a pretty name." I stroked
Paca's velvet nose and breathed in the comforting smell of
sweet hay and horses.

"She is quite a princess," Mama Tica said. "The name
Paca means 'free,' and she never lets me forget it. There we
go." She stood back up, dusting her hands. "She does not
like the saddle cinch, so she bloats her belly to make it

difficult for me to tighten it. It is a help to have someone to soothe her so she will relax. *Gracias*."

"*De nada*," I said. "You're welcome. Are you going riding?"

She adjusted Paca's bridle to fit smoother over one ear. "After the hard rains, I must check for bogs in the pasture. Would you like to come along?"

"Really?"

"I'm sure Cholo would like the exercise. Come. You can help me saddle him up."

Mama Tica tied Paca's lead to a post and asked me to get the saddle pad while she led Cholo from his stall. "You have done this before?"

"It was a long time ago," I admitted. "My grampa and gramma used to have horses."

"*Que bueno*. That is very nice."

I laid the saddle pad onto Cholo's back, and Mama Tica hefted the saddle and settled it into place. I was amazed she could do it so smoothly—those things weigh around fifty pounds. I always had to have my grampa help me when I went riding with him. Of course, I had been only nine at the time. . . .

Cholo didn't bother bloating up his belly, but stood stoically as Mama Tica tightened the cinch and adjusted the stirrups for me. Paca tossed her head and whinnied, as if to tell him he was being a wuss.

Mama Tica watched to make sure I could mount the saddle properly, then stepped up on Paca's stirrup and swung her leg over, settling gracefully into the seat. She made a clicking sound with her tongue, gently nudged Paca with her heels, and led the way out of the stable.

I was surprised to find that straddling a horse felt natural, as if it had been days instead of years since the last time I rode. My feet rested comfortably in the stirrups, and I sat tall and straight-backed in the saddle, just like I remembered. It took only a few strides for me to move with the steady side-to-side rhythm as Cholo walked behind Mama Tica and Paca.

A tiny bit of sun managed to slip through the clouds and danced on the dripping trees like moving spotlights. It hit the tips of the grass and then hid, flashed, and disappeared. It warmed my face for brief moments before hiding behind the clouds again——just enough for me to miss it when it was gone.

In the deep green field ahead of us, dozens of spotted cows stood in clusters, grazing, soaking in the brief rays of sunshine like I was or watching us silently with big, un-blinking doe eyes.

The trees of the cloud forest formed a towering backdrop.

"It is beautiful, isn't it?" Mama Tica asked. She had slowed Paca so that the horses were walking side by side. "My husband and I came here to manage the farm years ago, and we could never leave. We bought the place when it became available. Now he runs the dairy operation, and I look after the lodge."

"I can see why you would want to stay."

"Yes. Well, you must see many lovely places in your travels."

"We do," I admitted, "but this place feels like home."

Her smile lit her face like the sun. "I'm honored to hear you say this. We do try to work hard here, to provide a safe place to live the *pura vida*."

"Hard work? I thought *pura vida* meant having no worries, living in the moment, that kind of thing."

"Not exactly." She reigned in Paca and stopped next to me. "To have no worries does not mean to have no responsibilities. You first take care of your responsibilities, and then you may let go of your worries. To live *pura vida* is to take responsibility for yourself, for your actions, and to live the best life you can live. Understand?"

I nodded, but I couldn't answer because my guilt stuck in my throat like dry bread. Taking responsibility can be hard. It's easier to blame everyone else when things go wrong—like I did before I ran out of the lodge. It wasn't my fault someone had hacked into my blog, but it had been my responsibility to tell someone about it. I couldn't blame Liz for being angry after the network jumped on her case. Or Cavin. Or my mom and dad. Or Logan.

For days, I had been hiding the truth and worrying

about getting caught. If I'd have simply been honest, I could have let that worry go. Now I had the responsibility to make things right.

"I think I should get back," I said. I had a few apologies to make.

Mama Tica didn't ask questions, but clicked her tongue at Paca, and we turned the horses around. Not more than three steps into our return, Cholo started snorting and straining at the bit.

"Is he okay?" I worried. "I didn't turn him too hard, did I?"

Mama Tica shook her head and smiled. "The horses want to run once they realize we are headed back to the stables. Should we let them canter?"

Of course I said yes. It hardly seemed fair to the horses to tell them no. As soon as Cholo started running, though, I just about changed my mind. The balance was different. The rhythm was different. My first instinct was to grip the reins tighter, but I remembered how Grampa taught me to keep them loose in my hand. "Hold the reins too tight," he said, "and you'll pull the horse's head up so that it's uncomfortable for him to canter." The trick was to know when to let go.

After a minute, I found the flow, and I was able to relax. I loved the feeling of moving with the horse, like a dance in a fluid three-quarter beat, the breeze blowing back my hair. For the first time since I found that fake post on my blog,

I forgot to be worried or scared or guilty or any one thing, but let myself live in the joy of the moment. And I understood. This is what Mama Tica meant about the pure life. First, you had to learn how to live it.

Travel tip: It would be almost sacrilegious to visit Costa Rica without visiting one of the most active volcanoes in the world—Volcan Arenal.

The next morning, the entire group left before the sun came up to visit the Arenal Volcano. Logan practically sleepwalked to the SUV, and zonked right back out as soon as he hit the seat. I wanted to talk to him, but it could wait. Nothing was going to change in the time it took to drive to the lake where we would take a boat to get to the volcano.

Besides, if Man Rule Number One was not to try to talk to a guy while he's playing a game, Man Rule Number Something-way-up-there was not to try to talk to one when he wanted to sleep. (And never wake one up!)

Logan did have to get up for the boat ride, though. Claudia and Marco were filming us as we boarded, and we had to make it exciting! For about ten minutes anyway. Then I guess they decided they had all the on-the-boat footage they needed and wandered off to put the equipment away until we reached the other shore. But at least that was enough to ensure Logan was awake.

Mom and Dad's crew was filming an entire segment on the boat for *When in Rome*, though, so their cameras kept rolling long after our group quit. Which was okay by me— that meant they wouldn't be hovering.

"Huh," Logan said, fiddling with his phone. "Look at this." He held it out toward me, and at first I didn't know what he was talking about, but then I realized he was online. He had a signal!

I quickly pulled out my phone and found the right icons to push to access the Internet. And can I just say: Coolest. Thing. Ever. This was the first time I had ever been able to get online with my phone. I loved it.

"Weird that we can get a signal way out on the lake when we can't even get one at the farm," Logan said.

Victoria was standing nearby and must have heard us because she pointed to the trees along the shore. "You're picking up the cellular signal," she said, "from that tower."

I squinted, but I couldn't see what tower she was talking about.

"It's camouflaged," she explained. "Many companies try

to make their towers blend in with the environment. Do you notice that very straight tree just there?" She pointed again.

Then I could see it: a tree that matched the others in color, but it was too straight and symmetrical to be real.

"I'm rather surprised we're still within range," Victoria remarked. "I should think you won't have a signal much longer."

Logan and I exchanged a look, then immediately went for our phones' touch screens again. I'm not sure what he was looking up, but I logged onto the network website and then onto my blog. My stomach sank when I saw what was there. You guessed it. Another bogus post.

Cheesy, cheesy episode in the can, it said, boring hiking episode on the way. Can we go home now?

My hand trembled, holding my phone. I was right. It had to be someone local hacking into my account— someone who knew we had been to the cheese factory and that we were on our way to the volcano, where we were planning to hike up the mountain. I looked over to where my dad was cheerfully talking into the camera. He and my mom were not going to be happy to see the latest, especially since it meant that whoever it was had been able to get past the recent security changes. But I had to tell them, to be honest, like I promised.

"Um, Mom? Dad?" I called. "I need to show you something."

Cavin and my mom and dad managed to stay calm as everyone gathered around my phone, but Liz just about lost it. She yelled for the boat's captain to stop where we were so we wouldn't lose the signal, and then she whipped out her phone to call the network. Never mind that it was the middle of the night in New York.

I tried not to listen, but it was kind of hard since she was talking loud enough to be heard overseas. "I agree," she said, "if the sponsors believe we aren't on top of this thing, I'm afraid they will distance themselves." She paused and shot me a look, then turned her back to me and lowered her voice enough that I couldn't hear her words anymore. She paced to the other end of the boat, taking her discussion private. Mom and Dad and Cavin followed, but when I fell into step behind them, Dad shook his head.

"Not now, Cassidy," he said. Angrily. At least that's how it felt when he clipped his words like that.

When Liz got off the phone, all I could do was watch from a distance as the four of them discussed this latest development. As if I couldn't be trusted. But hadn't I told them immediately, just like I said I would? Why was I in trouble for telling the truth?

I stalked to the railing and stared out over the blue water, watching the volcano loom larger as we crossed the lake. I felt small. Helpless. Liz said the sponsors might distance themselves, and I got the feeling she thought it was my fault. What was I supposed to do? If the network's security couldn't stop the hacker, how could I? Unless . . .

Logan was sitting on one of the bench seats alone, playing with his phone. I rushed over to talk to him while no one was listening (after I made sure our lav mics were disconnected).

"I'm sorry," I blurted.

He tilted his head. "Go on."

"You were right. I should have trusted you enough to let you in on what was happening."

"I told you I would always be there for you, Cass," he said softly.

Heat crept along my cheeks and up the back of my neck as I remembered his saying that for the first time when we were in Spain together. "I know," I said. "It's just that it's been weird sometimes between us, you know?"

"I'm a guy," he said with a shrug. "We're annoying sometimes. What can I say?"

My face flushed again, only with embarrassment this time. "You heard that?"

His grin told me he had.

"Listen." I scooted closer to him and lowered my voice. "I made a mess of things, but now I want to make them right. And I can't do it by myself. I need my best friend to help me."

He pretended to consider it for a moment, and then he

asked, "Is there really a question? Of course I'll help you. Uh . . . to do what, exactly?"

We didn't get much of a chance to talk once we docked on the other side of the lake and began our hike through the Arenal Conservation Area to get a closer view of the volcano. Even in the midst of a crisis (as Liz called it), the show had to go on. Mom and Dad, Logan and I were wired with our lav mics and the cameras were rolling, making it very hard for us to plan what to do next.

Logan was the one who spotted another one of those cell-phone towers, and he signaled to me to pull out my phone.

What's your plan? he texted.

I slid a quick peek around to make sure no one was watching and texted back:

We find out exactly where these posts are coming from and figure out who's sending them.

Logan caught my eye and raised his shoulders, mouthing, How?

Britt, I typed. **She's the resident techie, right? I bet she knows how to dig around online.**

"Cassidy," Liz said sharply, "as pleased as I am for you to show your phones in use, we need you to be engaged in this hike or your viewers won't be."

Before I could come up with an appropriate response, something nearby roared, and I lost all rational thought. Okay, so it wasn't really a roar, but it was a horrible sound that I could only describe as a cross between a dog's bark and the yowl of a wounded lion.

I wasn't the only one it startled, either. Liz nearly dropped her tablet. "What was that?" she demanded.

The roar/bark/yowl came again, only longer this time. It raised goose bumps along my arms . . . but at least I wasn't freaking out like Britt was. She spun this way and that, trying to get a read on where the sound had come from, and then clung to Marco, burying her head in his shoulder. Smooth.

"Howler monkeys," Claudia said. "They are harmless."

"My, they are noisy," Victoria observed, her British accent very pronounced. Which is how I knew she was as unnerved by the noise as the rest of us non-*ticos*. "Where are they?"

Claudia and Marco trained the cameras up to the canopy, trying to catch a glimpse of the monkeys with their zoom lenses. I kept trying to follow the sound, but I couldn't see anything.

"There," Marco finally said, and pointed. "A pack of about a dozen or so in those branches."

I saw them immediately once I knew where to look. They weren't swinging through the leaves like I expected, but were literally hanging around, several of them draped like old blankets over the thick branches, and some lounging in the crooks of the trees. Little ones clung to their mothers or climbed over them like they were hairy jungle gyms. "Ooh, look," I said. "They've got babies."

"You see those?" Claudia pointed to a group of adults sitting with their legs folded beneath them. "They are eating guayaba fruits."

"Guava," Marco translated. "Don't worry," he told Britt gallantly, "the howlers are just warning us not to get too close. They will quiet down soon enough."

They did, but Britt still clung to Marco for the rest of the hike, as if we were in a savage jungle instead of a national park. Logan and I tried to pull her aside a couple of times, but it was clear she had no intention of leaving Marco for a moment.

"What should we do?" Logan whispered. "We're never going to get her alone."

I shrugged. "Wait, I guess. We can't do anything out here on the trail anyway. We're staying at that resort tonight. Maybe we can catch her there."

With our tentative plan in place, I was able to relax a little and enjoy the rest of the hike to the volcano. Even with Liz reminding us every ten minutes, Smile! Look into the camera! Point out those orchids!

At least she quieted down a little when the trail got steeper. And rougher. As we hiked higher up the mountain, trees gave way to black volcanic rock.

"Arenal has been active until recently," Marco told us, "with lava flows almost daily at times. It is sleeping for now, but even so, we are not allowed to hike beyond the observation point. The volcano is still seismically active, and new magma supplies could erupt again at any time."

He hiked on ahead of us, moving faster up the hill instead of slowing down. His focus ahead reminded me of Mama Tica's horses when they knew they were headed for the barn. Marco knew what waited for us up ahead, and he couldn't wait to get there.

I signaled to Logan. "Come on!"

We caught up to Marco just as the trail began to flatten out. And as we crested the last rise, I knew why Marco had been in such a hurry to get there. In front of us, Arenal swooped upward in a perfect cone, its peak crowned by a halo of clouds. At its base stretched green lowlands for miles and miles. A deep blue lagoon was carved into the valley on one side of the mountain.

"Breathtaking, isn't it?" Victoria said.

I looked back to where Liz was still laboring up the final stretch of trail, puffing like the little engine who could. I smiled. "Yes, it is."

Claudia, Estefan, and Bayani all set up cameras to try to capture the view. I didn't even bother taking out my phone because I knew that no pictures would ever do it justice. I could have stayed up there all afternoon, but the clouds at the top of Arenal were sinking steadily lower, and growing darker. Finally, Marco decided we should make our way back down the mountain before the rain set in.

I took one last look at Arenal and the valley below to save it in my memory, then turned to follow Marco down the trail.

That night, we stayed at a hotel resort with an amazing view of Arenal and natural hot springs on the property. Logan and I planned to corner Britt in the hot springs and to convince her to help us catch my blog intruder. Once we found out where the hacked messages were coming from, I could turn the evidence over to my mom and dad, and maybe then they would stop acting as if I couldn't be trusted. I changed into my bathing suit and hurried down to the springs to see if Britt was there yet.

When I walked out onto the wooden pathway, the first thing I noticed was the smell. I've been to other geothermal hot springs in other places, and a lot of times you get a rotten-egg kind of sulfur stink from the water, but all I smelled from these springs was the rich, earthy smell of dirt and damp.

The next thing I noticed was the steam. It rose in writhing wisps from the springs and then hung in the cool night air like the clouds in Monteverde.

Logan and his dad were in the closest pool, lounging

against a rocky ledge, but beyond that, I couldn't see anyone. All the other pools were veiled by the steam.

I draped my towel on the handrail at the side of Logan's
pool and stepped down into the water. Then immediately
back out again. "It's hot!"

"Yeah," Logan said in his duh tone. "That's why they
call it a hot spring."

"No, I mean it's really hot. How are you not boiling
in there?"

Logan pushed away from the ledge and waded toward
me in the waist-deep water. "Don't be such a baby. It's not
that hot. Come in."

He reached a hand out to help me into the water. It was
an innocent gesture, and I knew he probably didn't mean
anything by it, but it made my heart melt just the same. I
took his hand and stepped into the scalding water.

Okay, so it wasn't really scalding. It *was* hot, but after
I took the first couple of steps, it didn't seem that bad.
Probably not much hotter than a Jacuzzi. Actually, it was a
pretty good bet I was hotter inside than the water outside
because Logan was *holding my hand*! He could have let it
go as soon as I made it down the steps without falling, but
he didn't.

I tried to be as casual about it as he was. Looking at
him, you wouldn't guess holding hands was anything out
of the ordinary. Meanwhile, I was quietly hyperventilating.

And so, of course, I started to babble like I always do when I'm excited or nervous.

"Can you see the volcano from here? Have you seen my mom and dad? What about Britt? Where is everyone?"

He led me over to the side where he had been sitting with his dad before letting go of my hand. "Haven't seen anything. Da says the clouds are too low tonight because it's going to rain again, but I can't really see if it's cloudy in the dark sky."

I gazed upward. "Well, I don't see any stars, so it's a pretty good guess there are clouds in the way."

"Could be the steam from the hot springs," he reasoned.

"Which cooled and condensed and became clouds," I said.

"Clever."

"Plus," I added, "can steam do this?" I put my hand out to catch a raindrop. It was cool against my skin.

The rain started slowly at first, just a few drips here and there, but then it was falling faster and faster until the drops were coming down in a steady beat. Logan threw his head back and opened his mouth, his tongue sticking out.

"Ew." I wrinkled my nose. "What if that water fell through miles of pollution?"

"It didn't," Logan said. "And even if it did, I don't care. I love the rain." He threw his arms open and turned in a slow circle. This time I followed his lead. Soon we were both laughing and dancing in the hot water, our arms outspread to catch the cool rain.

I thought to myself what a simple thing it was, appreciating rain. Yet here we were, happy just to feel the water on our faces. And content. And, for the moment, completely worry-free.

Until the rain stopped again.

Then everything came flooding back to me and I remembered why I had rushed down to the hot springs in the first place. "Come on," I told Logan, "we have to find Britt."

We climbed out of the pool we were in to cross to another spring-fed pool. Instantly, I shivered as the air chilled my skin. I practically jumped into the next pool just to be warm again. We looked through four pools before we saw Britt flirting with Marco near a natural waterfall. Of course.

Logan and I waded toward them. We were both making plenty of noise, but neither Britt nor Marco seemed to hear us. In fact, Britt jumped when we got close enough to call her name.

She glared at us—clearly we had interrupted something—and asked sharply, "What is it?"

I hesitated. We needed her on our side if we were going to rely on her help. Starting off the conversation on her bad side was not part of the game plan. Neither was including Marco in our confidence.

"Uh . . . could we talk to you for a minute?" I asked.

She gave me a look that could boil the water we were standing in. "Ex*cuse* me," she snapped. "Busy."

"But we just wanted to ask you—" Logan began.

I took his arm to pull him away. "It's no use," I told him in a low voice. "She's not a team player."

We left Britt with Marco. "You have a plan B?" Logan asked.

I didn't. I'd been counting on Britt because she seemed like the logical person to turn to, but now . . .

"Hey, guys," Bayani called. "Hot enough for you?"

Logan and I exchanged a quick look. Bayani. Of course! If we had to rely on an adult (or in Bayani's case, a semiadult) he was the perfect choice. He was connected enough to help, but just rebellious enough not to tell on us.

"Yans," Logan said in a low voice, "can we talk?"

We explained the situation to Bayani, and he listened with a serious expression on his face. Given that he likes to tease me so much, I was afraid he'd give us a hard time, but he just nodded and grunted once in a while until we were done.

"Okay, listen," he said. "I got a friend who can maybe help out with this. Total computer geek. If there's a way of tracking down who posted those entries, he can find it. But Cassidy? It's not going to change anything. You got that, right?"

No, I didn't *get* it. I mean, if we solved the problem, why wouldn't that change *everything*? "What are you talk-ing about?"

"The sponsors are spooked." He looked out over the steamy water for a moment and then back at us with the most serious look on his face I had seen since . . . forever. "You've seen how people make up their own stories out of what they think they see, right? Even though half the viewers know in their brains that they're being manipulated by reality shows, some part of them wants to believe the juicy stuff. So even if you flash the truth in front of them in neon greens and pinks, they're going to believe what they want to believe, whatever's the most entertaining."

Logan laughed. "Greens and pinks?"

"I'm making a point here," Bayani said with a sniff. But he grinned just the same.

"I don't see what's so funny," I said. "You're telling me that no matter what I do, people are going to think the worst of me because it's more *entertaining*?"

"Pretty much, yeah," Bayani said.

"But it's obvious I didn't write that stuff!" I protested.

"Right. Everybody knows that," he said.

"Then I don't get what you're saying." Really. He wasn't making any sense.

"The gossip they're running with isn't that you wrote those nasty things, but that you're out of control." I was about to protest, but he raised his hand to stop me. "Not *you*, you. The *show*. Like, if we can't even control content, how can we control two teenagers?"

"Two?" Logan laughed and punched Bayani in the arm. "You mean I'm included in this scandal or whatever? *Craic*."

I slapped a handful of water at Logan. "I don't know what you're so happy about. This isn't funny."

"I don't know," Bayani said. "In a way it is. They're casting Logan as the bad boy in this opera."

Logan laughed again, and I glared at him. "How do they even know who Logan is?" I asked Bayani. "The shows haven't started yet."

"But the prepub has," he said, and then corrected himself. "Well, it had. Before this all hit the fan. Now I think the sponsors are trying to lie low until they see where public opinion goes. So far it's been focused on your unsupervised lifestyles."

I snorted (which, I admit, was not very attractive). "Unsupervised? Ha!"

"Again, reality doesn't matter," Bayani said. "It's cooler to believe you two are running amok."

"Amok," Logan chuckled. "I love it."

"Listen." I turned my back on Logan and tried to reason with Bayani. "If we can find out who was posting those messages and turn the story around, we can win the sponsors back, right?"

"Well, sure," he said. "They want to be on the winning

team. So you convince your public that you're a hero, and the sponsors will fight to be a part of that."

"So that's what we need to do." I linked arms with Bayani and Logan. "We have to become heroes."

Now I just had to figure out how we were going to do that.

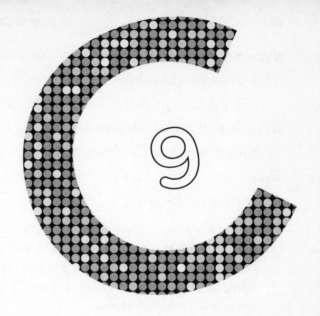

I slept better that night than I had all week. After the hike to the volcano and our soak in the hot springs, I was so tired I was out almost before I hit the pillow. But it was more than just being physically exhausted. My brain was drained as well. All that worrying and wondering and secretly plotting took more out of me than I expected. That part I was able to turn off, though, now that I knew Bayani would help us. It's like we passed the weight of it to him for a while, so I could finally relax.

I woke to my phone buzzing and nearly fell out of bed reaching to grab for it. Zoe's face flashed on the screen, and my breath caught for an instant. The last thing I needed was another bad blog report. I rubbed my eyes to focus on the message and sighed with relief. Nothing about the blog. This was an update about Nikos.

Since I left them in Greece, Zoe and Nikos had become best friends, just like Logan and me. Well, almost like Logan and me. The difference is that Zoe knows Nikos likes her as more than a friend, and that's something I can never tell with Logan.

> Am at my diving invitational, Zoe texted. Nikos is here, and all the girls stare at him in the stands. I have to tell my teammates to think of the competition or we will lose, but still it is hard for them not to watch Nikos.

> Well, yeah, I texted back. He's only a movie star's son. And completely adorable. What's not to stare at?

> Zoe texted a smiley face and then wrote, I know, yes? At first I worry about the attention, but when he waves to me from the stands, I feel proud that the other girls stare. Is that bad?

> I laughed and typed, Not bad at all. But now you know you don't have to worry so much.

Which is the same thing Logan said to me the night before. There was nothing to worry about. Bayani's friend would track down our villain, I could do one of those public-apology posts on my blog that my followers seemed to like so much, and Logan and I would show the sponsors how in control we could be. Everything was going to be fine. Better than fine. This whole episode could actually turn out to be a good thing, like Nikos waving from the stands. I couldn't have been more wrong.

The first hint I got that something was up was when Bayani didn't show for breakfast. Britt said he had probably slept in, but that wasn't like Bayani; he's usually one of the first people at the table when there's food involved. Plus, since he's the fixer, he has to get an early start to make sure all arrangements are in place. I checked his room anyway, just to be sure, but he wasn't there.

"Don't worry," Logan told me. "Da said Yans took the early ferry this morning and that he'd meet us back at the farm. Probably, you know, checking into . . . the situation."

He was right, of course, but I couldn't shake the niggling doubt in my gut. Which didn't help on the ride back across the lake when Liz wanted footage of Logan and me looking carefree and outdoorsy in our sponsor-provided boating attire.

"Talk to each other," she instructed. "Show us that you're having a good time. Cassidy, dearest, could you at least try to smile?"

I did my best to grimace in a way that made the corners of my mouth turn up, but I probably didn't succeed, because Liz finally called it a morning and let Estefan and Claudia go for the rest of the ride. I suppose I should have felt bad, but she said she wanted real, and the reality was, I was scared.

It was one thing to ask Bayani to help track down a hacker, but it was quite another to think he actually may have found something. Once we knew who the hacker was, what then? Ask him/her to stop? Demand whatever tabloid he or she worked with to leave me alone? That would only create a bigger story. Maybe I should have let it go.

The anticipation got worse when Bayani wasn't waiting at the farm when the rest of us got there. Logan tried calling Bayani's cell, but, of course, the farm was one huge dead zone, and he couldn't get a signal.

I paced and twisted my hands. "What if something happened to him?"

Logan didn't even say the words. He just gave me a look. I worried too much.

Victoria strolled up beside us with her lesson folders nestled in the crook of her arm. "All right, you two," she said. "What are you scheming about?"

I jumped back from Logan as if I was actually guilty of something, but he didn't flinch. "Just talking about our research animals. I'm saying a spider money could take a tapir in a fight any day. What do you think?"

"I think your evasion technique is just a tad unrefined. Now come along. Let's get started before the camera crew arrives to distract you from your schoolwork."

We followed her to the conference room but didn't even get a chance to sit down before Bayani slipped through the door, closing it carefully behind him like he was afraid to make a sound. "Sorry for interrupting," he told Victoria. "I need to talk with Cassidy and Logan for a minute."

"That's fine," she said. "Go ahead."

He rubbed his palms against his pants nervously and cleared his throat. "Alone."

Victoria crossed her arms. "I don't know what's going on here, but Cassidy hasn't been herself all morning, and Logan checked out before he stepped inside this room. As their tutor, I think I have a right to be let into the little circle of conspirators we have here."

Bayani looked to me for confirmation, which I have to admit scared me a little bit. He's always joking around and full of himself, and he never defers to me. Seeing him like this made the hairs at the nape of my neck start to itch. I nodded to him; of the four of us in the room, Victoria was the most practical and level-headed. If Bayani was losing it, we needed Victoria on our team.

"You're going to want to sit for this," he said. He took a chair from the conference table and turned it around so that he could straddle it, facing us. "Okay, so. I told you my geek buddy could track down anything, right? So he worked his tech-guy magic, or whatever, to track down our hacker and . . ." He looked around like he expected someone to crash through the walls and bash him on the head. Then he leaned forward over the back of the chair and lowered his voice to a whisper. "Whoever hacked into Cassidy's account was doing it from right here."

"I knew it!" I thought of all the eyes I felt watching me the past couple of days, and I shivered. "So are we talking here as in Costa Rica, or here as in Monteverde?"

"Here," Bayani repeated, pointing to the ground. "I mean your hacker is right here, at the farm."

I heard the words, but they didn't compute. "But . . . the Internet has been down the whole time we've been here. I know; I've tried to connect. Mama Tica even said—"

"All I can tell you," Bayani said, "is that my guy isolated the IP address, and it was assigned to a computer here at their office address."

"Wait a minute." Victoria held up both hands like a London traffic cop. "Back it up. What's this about?"

"I want to find out who's been hacking into my blog," I explained. "Maybe then we can convince the sponsors this isn't going to be an ongoing thing, and they don't have to pull out."

"I see. And you're encouraging this, Bayani?"

"Hey." He raised his hands defensively. "Not my idea. I just did what they asked me." Then, as if he realized how lame that must sound, he added, "I didn't know we'd actually come up with a location. I figured anyone good enough to get past network security would have routed their input through proxy servers or something so they couldn't be found. I thought if we came up with a goose egg, Cassidy and Logan would forget this crazy idea of catching the perp and let it go."

Victoria raised her eyebrows. "We've gone from an anonymous hacker to a perpetrator now? Don't you realize you are encouraging them?"

"Look," Bayani said evenly, "it was different when I thought of this person as some anonymous, faceless entity. But if he—or she—is here among us, it's personal. It goes beyond showing the world how clever you are because you can get around a firewall or two. Now we're talking sabotage."

I gasped, remembering how some of the posts were written as if the hacker knew my every move. And no wonder, if he or she was living among us.

Victoria took one look at my face and shot out of her seat. "All right. That's it," she told Bayani. "We should discuss this outside."

"No!" I grabbed her hand. "This is about me. My blog. I want to hear what he has to say."

"Cassidy, I'm afraid you three are building on one another's paranoia. And Bayani, I don't think that isolating one IP address is enough to pinpoint a location."

He shrugged. "I'm not really sure how it works. That's why I have smart friends. Like you."

She pressed her lips together. "How kind," she said drily. "Now, if you'll excuse me, I'll go fetch Liz and we can—"

"No!" I jumped up after her. "No Liz. You heard what she said. If she even suspects my blog can be hacked into again, she'll call off the show."

Victoria paused. She had heard Liz's lecture on the boat just as well as the rest of us. "Cavin, then," she said. "Or your mum and dad."

"They're all in town," Logan reminded her. "We can't sit around and do nothing while they're gone."

"Let's just look for the source," I said. "If we can find the one working computer on the farm, then we know we're on the right track."

"Or completely offtrack," Victoria muttered.

"But you'll help us" I asked hopefully, "to narrow down the list of suspects?"

"I'll help you," she said, "not to make fools of yourselves by accusing innocent people."

With Liz and the cameras on their way at any moment, we didn't have much time to argue the different possibilities.

"Okay," I said, "the way I see it, we have three main suspects: Marco, Claudia, and Estefan."

"And Mama Tica," Bayani added.

I shook my head to keep his words out. "No. No way."

"Well, it is her place," Logan said.

"She wouldn't do that," I said firmly.

"How do you know?"

I stared him down. It was a fair enough question, but I didn't know how to explain. What was I going to say—I know it can't be Mama Tica because she reminds me of my gramma? It sounded lame when you said it like that, but it was the truth. Some things you know. "I just do, that's all. Let's concentrate on the ones who really could have done it."

"Someone with the means, opportunity, and motive," Victoria put in.

"The what?"

"It's how detectives narrow down their list of suspects. Are they capable of the crime? Could they have done it? What would compel them to do so?"

"Any of them could be capable," Bayani said, "but why would they want to mess with your blog?"

"One of the tabloids could be paying them for a story," I suggested.

"Perhaps," Victoria allowed, "but I don't know when you think any of these people on your list would have had the opportunity. It can be time-consuming to get through the network's security and firewalls. We've all been together most of the time."

"*Most* of the time," Bayani repeated ominously.

Victoria shot him a look, but continued. "If it will put your mind at ease, perhaps we should watch these three over the next couple of days. See if anything about their behavior warrants suspicion."

"Good idea," Bayani agreed enthusiastically. "No one knows about the tracking but us, so they won't know we're watching."

Victoria folded her arms. "You, sir, are enjoying this entirely too much."

"Why not?" he asked. "Haven't you figured out yet that drama is fun?"

I was pretty sure Bayani was joking, but I hoped he remembered that attitude. Because I had the feeling that if we went ahead with our amateur investigation, we had a lot of "fun" in store for us.

Travel tip: Costa Rica possesses about 5 percent of the total world's biodiversity. Remember that this biodiversity extends into the insect world.

The next day, since it was only drizzling instead of full-on raining, we decided to go ahead with the cloud forest walk that kept getting postponed.

Logan and I had to figure out how not to let our sponsor's clothing gifts get completely covered up by our mandatory rain slickers. I had to come to terms with being filmed wearing rubber farm boots. Daniel did my hair special for the combination of rain and humidity by pulling it back into two French braids that merged into one at the nape of my neck. The style showed off my new Marc earrings.

"Do you like it?" he asked proudly when he was done.

I assured him that I did, but to be honest, he could have teased my hair into a full bouffant and I wouldn't have known any different. I was too busy watching my suspects and formulating theories. I was anxious to see if Bayani, Logan, or Victoria came up with anything similar.

I had concentration issues on the tour as well, and after being scolded by Liz a dozen times to look "engaged," I finally signaled the rest of the group that it was time for a break. While everyone else took five, I grabbed Logan, Bayani, and Victoria and told them we needed to talk. *Now*. We ducked behind a big tree to discuss what we'd found.

Logan and I unplugged our lavs and bent our heads together. "I'm telling you, it's Claudia," I insisted. "She's so emotionless."

"Yes, but Estefan is always watching everyone," Logan said. "Watching, watching, watching. It's kind of creepy."

"Or it could be Marco," Bayani put in. "Why is he always casing out the farm? Suspicious."

"He's not casing out anything," Victoria argued. "He's walking. Getting exercise. There's a difference."

"Oh, there you are!"

We all jumped in unison and turned around to find Liz standing behind us in her jungle khakis, with her hands on her hips and a perplexed look on her face. "Do I want to know what you four are up to?"

"We're just checking out this bromeliad," Logan said without missing a beat. "There's a frog in it. Look."

I found his hand and squeezed it. Nice save.

He nodded toward the bright red plant, and I looked

closer, catching my breath. There really was a little frog nestled among the leaves. I had to hide my surprise since I was supposed to have been already looking at it, so I couldn't show how awed I was. The colors of the little guy were incredible. He had crimson-red eyes and tiny orange feet with a little round sucker at the tip of each toe. His back was leaf green, but his sides were blue like Arenal Lake in the sunlight.

"It looks like a red-eyed leaf frog," Victoria said, slipping right back into lesson mode. "Notice how well it blends in with its environment."

Which was true. You wouldn't think that anything so colorful would blend in instead of stand out, but in the cloud forest, where everything was green, with random bursts of color, he was perfectly camouflaged.

"Well, I'll be," Liz cooed, and then yelled over her shoulder, "Claudia! Marco! Here!"

"Shh," Victoria reminded her. "We don't want to get too close."

Immediately, everyone in the group hovered around, pointing out the tree frog, talking about the tree frog, filming the tree frog. And while they watched the tree frog, I watched them, looking for a tell, a sign—anything that would give the hacker away. Marco glanced up as I was studying him, and suddenly his face changed, became a complete blank.

The tree frog quickly had enough of being examined and hopped off to hide among the leaves. Once it was gone, Marco suggested we come see the quetzal bird he and Claudia had been filming earlier. Everyone filed back up the trail except for Liz, who hung back to bring up the rear. I was second to last.

"Strange," she mused as she walked behind me, "how your mics keep hitting dead spots. I do hope we won't have to resort to having Claudia follow you around with a boom. That would be most inconvenient."

"Absolutely," I said. "I couldn't agree more."

I hurried ahead of her, my footsteps muffled by the spongy moss on the cloud forest floor. Liz made me nervous. Wouldn't it be weird if *she* was actually the one who hacked into my account? It was an intriguing thought, since she was a very unlikely suspect.

I had just about caught Victoria to tell her my addition to the suspect pool when she cried out, and then limped over to lean against a tree, obviously in pain.

"What's the matter?" I hurried over to her to see if I could help. "Did you twist your ankle?"

She pressed her lips into a thin straight line and shook her head. "Bite," she managed to say. "Something bit me."

My hands went cold. At the beginning of the walk, Marco had warned us about turning over rocks or even leaves and potentially disturbing a poisonous snake or a spider or even a dart frog. What if whatever bit Victoria was poisonous?

"Marco!" I yelled. "We need help!" Even though he was a top suspect, he was our guide and knew the forest well. He would know what to do.

Sure enough, in no time, he rushed back down the trail to look at Victoria's foot, carefully peeling back her sock. "It's a spider bite all right. From the size of the punctures, I'd guess a wanderer. You didn't happen to see it, did you?"

Victoria shook her head. Her face had gone gray.

"Probably not much to worry about aside from the pain," Marco assured her. "Except for allergies. You're not allergic to anything, are you?"

Victoria closed her eyes and took a deep breath before answering. "Yes."

"What are you allergic to?"

She looked down at her foot. "Spider bites."

10

"Are you sure you're going to be all right?" I asked for about the tenth time that morning.

Mama Tica had given Victoria some antihistamine pills when we returned to the farm and had offered to call a doctor, but Victoria, in true Victoria fashion, insisted she'd be fine. That night, she had been unable to sleep because her foot was throbbing, but she didn't want to disturb anyone, so she quietly soaked her foot in the hopes that the swelling would go down. It didn't. By morning, it was clear she had a serious problem on her hands.

She was trying to hobble down the stairs when my mom saw her and sounded the alarm. Within minutes, the entire group gathered in the front room, where Victoria had managed to make it to a chair, and arrangements were quickly made to have the bite looked at.

"Does it hurt bad?" I asked.

"I'm fine," she said again, not even bothering to correct my grammar. That omission told me much more than her words.

I shot a panicked look toward my dad, and he hooked one hand around the back of his neck. "That's it," he said, "we're going to cancel the segment for today and go with you to the hospital."

"Please don't," Victoria said. "I'll be fine. We have only a few days left in Costa Rica, and you need to take advantage of the break in the clouds while you can."

"Got the insurance information," Bayani said, waving the piece of paper to prove it. "Estefan has gone to pull up the car."

"I really wish you wouldn't make a fuss," Victoria said to no one in particular. Maybe she was talking to her foot, which had swollen to nearly twice its size.

Liz handed Bayani one of the camcorders. "Don't forget the camera."

I gaped at her. "You're kidding, right?" I mean, I knew drama was good TV, but this was real, not "reality."

Bayani took the camcorder from Liz and pointedly set it down on the couch. "This is not part of your show." Then, ignoring Liz's sputtering, he calmly folded up the insurance paper and tucked it into the pocket of his jeans.

Victoria took my hand. "Now I expect you and Logan to have your research-paper outlines done by the time I get back. I don't anticipate it will be long, so be sure to use your time judiciously."

"Now *you're* kidding," I accused.

"Not in the least. Your three hours is a requirement, regardless of the circumstances. Claudia has agreed to step in as your tutor this morning."

My jaw dropped. Claudia? But she was one of our chief hacker suspects.

Victoria gave me a steely look, as if she could tell what I was thinking. "Claudia can be a valuable resource to you, with her native perspective. You will be wise to learn what you can from her while you have the opportunity."

"All right," Cavin announced, "the car's out front."

Victoria pushed herself out of the chair. "Right. Here we go, then."

Dad and Daniel flanked her on either side, and she slung an arm around each of their shoulders to take the weight off her foot. Together, they made slow progress out the front door. Mama Tica followed with an armload of pillows to make Victoria comfortable on the long ride to the hospital. The rest of us trailed behind helplessly, wanting to do something but not knowing what it would be.

"My, what a production," Victoria said as they helped her into the backseat of the SUV and situated the pillows around her.

"She's so British," I told Logan as we watched her trying to keep that "stiff upper lip" she was so proud of, even though her lips had gone completely white, like the rest of her face. I hoped her treatment at the hospital included some kind of pain meds.

The doors shut, closing Victoria away from us, and the SUV pulled away. Those of us left behind huddled together, watching the SUV bump away down the long driveway and turn onto the main road.

Once it was out of sight, Claudia cleared her throat. "Well, then," she said to Logan and me, "should we start your class now or later?"

"Later," Mama Tica answered for us. "You've none of you had breakfast. Come inside and eat. The day looks better on a full stomach."

At the dining-room table, I picked at my *gallo pinto* and eggs. "You really think she'll be all right?"

Mom rubbed my back. "Honey, Victoria's too stubborn to have it any other way. They'll give her some medicine and antibiotics, and she'll be fine."

"I wish we could have gone with her."

"And what good would that have done? We'd only clog the waiting room and make things difficult for the hospital staff. It's best we keep out of the way. Bayani's with her. He'll make sure she's comfortable."

I picked at my rice. "I could have done that," I muttered.

"I'm sure you would have," Dad said gently. "And if you were of legal age to sign admission papers, we would have sent you before anyone else."

"Excuse me." Cavin stood by my mom's chair, holding a sheet of paper in his hand. "When you have a moment, we need to go through the changes to the schedule this morning."

As my mom and dad turned to talk with Cavin, Logan slipped onto the chair next to mine. "We've got to get out of class this morning," he whispered.

I stole a quick glance at my mom and dad, and then answered in a low voice, "Sounds good to me. Why?"

"I heard Estefan and Marco talking. There's a spot out in the pasture where you can get cell reception."

"Okay," I said slowly. I mean, I was glad to hear it and everything, but what did it have to do with class?

"Maybe there didn't need to be an active Internet connection this week. Someone could have used a smartphone to post those blog entries. We should go check it out."

I looked over my shoulder to make sure no one was standing close to us and then whispered, "I thought Bayani said the IP address was Finca Calderón's office."

"I dunno," he said. "They could have routed it with a phone, right?"

"Yeah. So how do we get out of—"

"Hey, you two," Cavin said. "What're you cooking up over there? Ye look entirely too conspiratorial for my taste."

"Da!" Logan glared at his dad, and if I didn't know he was covering for the fact that we actually *were* conspiring, I would have thought he was really mad.

Cavin laughed and threw his hands up in mock surrender. "Kids," he said to my parents, chuckling. He opened his mouth like he was going to say more, but then closed it again and watched us sharply.

"Hmm," he said again. "Kids."

Logan and I sat in the conference room with books and pamphlets spread on the table, studiously copying down information for our reports. I had it all worked out how we were going to get Claudia to let us go early by offending her no-nonsense, anti-emotional nature with a crying jag over Victoria's plight, but then Liz came along and ruined everything.

She poked her head into the room and announced, "Oh, good. You've gotten a head start. Britt will be along shortly."

"Britt?" I asked. "But I thought Claudia was—"

"Change of plans. Claudia will be riding along with the *When in Rome* crew. They need a guide, and both Estefan and Bayani are with Victoria. It was a toss-up between Claudia and Marco, and Marco volunteered to stay with our crew, so Claudia won."

"Doesn't Britt usually go with the *When in Rome* crew?" Logan asked.

Liz sighed. "Yes, she does. But after Victoria's unfortunate experience yesterday, Britt is disinclined to venture into the cloud forest again, so she'll be sitting in the classroom with you."

I almost hated to bring it up because Liz was already looking so frazzled, but I raised my hand anyway. "Um, Liz?"

She leaned her head against the doorframe. "Yes?"

"If Britt's our teacher today and she doesn't want to go into the cloud forest, how are we going to do the shoot this afternoon? We're supposed to have a teacher with us at all—"

"Yes. Thank you, Cassidy," Liz said, pinching the bridge of her nose. "I am well aware of the regulations. Which is why, while you are in class, I will be on the phone, trying to arrange an alternate location where Britt will be more comfortable accompanying us. Now, if there is nothing else . . . ?"

"Naw, we're good," Logan said. "Thanks."

When she was gone, he shut his book and leaned back in his chair. "What's Britt going to do the rest of the trip if she won't go into the forest?"

I just shook my head and laughed.

"What's so funny?" Logan asked.

"I know why Britt wanted to stay behind, and it doesn't have anything to do with spiders."

He raised his brows and gestured for me to continue.

"Didn't you hear what Liz said?" I asked. "Marco is staying here. Britt has a thing for Marco, so . . ."

"Ah. Britt is pretending to be traumatized by last night so she can stay at the farm with Marco."

I smiled. "Exactly. Which should make it supereasy to convince her to let us out of class early."

"Because . . . ?" Logan prodded.

"Hello? She wants to spend time with Marco, not us. We simply need to let her know we're perfectly fine with that arrangement."

Britt didn't even pretend to try to teach us anything. She showed up twenty minutes after Liz had come in to check on us, and then she just sat around, staring out the window or doodling in her notebook. Probably writing Marco's name with lots of swirly letters and hearts all around. I don't know because she was hiding whatever it was behind her hand.

I swear, she was acting like a seventh grader with a major crush. I'll admit I don't know a whole lot about how most seventh graders act because I spent only about three weeks in middle school while I was in Ohio, but I saw a lot of seventh-grade drama then, and from what I could tell, Britt would fit right in.

Logan kept drumming his pencil on the table and making big gestures with his eyes, by which I'm pretty sure he meant I should start trying to convince Britt that it would be a good idea for us all to ditch class. I made faces back, because I wasn't really planning on doing all the talking. I was kind of counting on his helping me.

But if I didn't say something, we'd still be sitting there when Liz got done with her phone calls and came to announce where we'd be filming that day, and then who knew when we'd have another opportunity to slip away?

I raised my hand, but Britt didn't notice me. She kept staring at her paper with a goofy smile on her face.

"Excuse me, Britt?"

She slapped her hand over the writing and looked up at me. "What?"

Logan and I exchanged a quick glance, and then I rushed ahead. "Well, we're doing nature research papers and it's such a nice day right now, we were wondering if maybe we could go outside to work on them?"

"To soak up the nature," Logan added helpfully.

"Oh. I don't know. What does Victoria do?"

It was almost too easy. I really had to concentrate to keep from smiling. "She likes to have lessons outside." Which was true.

Britt considered that for a moment. "But you're not talking about doing a lesson, are you?"

I frowned. Maybe it wasn't going to be as easy as I thought. "Well, no, but we'd be working on our papers."

"I understand. You don't want to be here." She stared wistfully out the window. "I don't blame you, but the regulations say three hours of class time each day."

"Yeah, but it doesn't say those three hours have to be in a *classroom*," I countered.

"Right," Logan said, "it's three hours of learning time. If we're working on our papers, we're learning."

"I don't know," she said, even though we all knew letting us go is what she wanted to do. "You promise to work on your papers?"

"I guarantee we'll be doing research," I said.

"All right then," she said, clearly relieved. "Class dismissed."

Travel tip: In general, Costa Ricans are very affectionate and are often physically expressive, even in public.

"Where are you kids off to?" Mama Tica caught Logan and me just as we were about to go out the door.

"Research." I said. "Outside."

I couldn't look at her when I said that. It wasn't a lie, but I still felt as though we were deceiving Mama Tica. She deserved more respect than that. In fact, I almost broke down and confessed the whole thing, but she saved me by saying, "Well, you certainly can't go out without boots. The ground is muddy, and the grass is wet." She pointed to a cabinet by the door where she stored the ubiquitous black rubber farm boots. "Put them on first, then you may go outside."

We both obeyed gratefully and escaped before the guilt could set in.

"So where did they say they could get the signal?" I asked Logan. "It's a pretty big property."

"They said something about a south pasture," Logan answered. "Do you know where that is?"

"Are you kidding? I get all turned around in new places. I don't even know which way is south."

"That much is easy." He squinted up at the sky. "The sun rises in the east, and it's about nine o'clock, so this way"—he faced toward the sun—"is east. Which means this way"—he took a quarter turn to his right— "would be south."

I knew that. "Okay," I said, "so the pasture is this way. Did they say *where* in the pasture?"

"I didn't hear specific directions," he said. "But we'll find it. Just hold your phone out and watch for connectivity bars."

As luck would have it, the south pasture sat on a hilly slope overlooking the rest of the farm. Which would account for it being the one place where you could find a cell-phone signal. But it also meant that getting up to it was a hike.

I kept watching for any bars on my phone, but the search signal kept spinning around and around. . . . Logan didn't appear to be having any better luck.

The long grass was still wet from the morning dew. Or maybe it was from the rain. All I know is, I was glad for the boots, fashionable or not. I thanked Mama Tica under my breath for insisting we wear them.

"What did you say?" Logan asked.

"Nothing," I puffed beside him. Why wasn't he getting winded from the climb? I resolved to add a workout to my daily routine. No way was I going to let him show me up everywhere we went.

At the top of the slope, a group of cows stood watching us, unblinking, flicking their tails, slowly chewing, their jaws working in a kind of up-and-down and side-to-side movement that was strangely mesmerizing.

Suddenly, Logan grabbed me and yanked me toward him. "Watch out!" My rubber boots slipped in the wet grass and I almost went down, but Logan caught me and propped me up. "You just about stepped in . . . that." He pointed to what my gramma would call a cow pie. Well, we *were* in a pasture.

Now I remembered the other reason people on farms wear boots. "Thanks," I told him sincerely.

He set me back on my feet and let go. I wondered about the merits of slipping again.

"Okay," I said instead, "we're at the top. Are you getting anything?"

He shook his head and turned his phone to show me. Nothing. "We'll probably just have to walk around to find the sweet spot."

Well, I decided, I could think of worse things. The view from the top of the hill was incredible, with the farm spread out below us. Beyond that, green, rolling hills met with the deeper green of the lush trees in the forest. A mist hung in the lowest-lying areas, giving the whole scene a soft-focus feel. Meanwhile, on the hill, the sun felt warm on my skin, but not too warm. Just enough to offset the morning chill. And, of course, I had Logan beside me. If it wasn't for the cow smell swirling around us on the breeze, it would have been a perfect moment.

"Have you ever seen such a—"

"I got it!" Logan interrupted. He was holding his phone up about shoulder height and pointing it due east. (I could tell from the angle of the sun. Thank you, Logan.) "Three bars."

I checked my phone as well and found that I had four. "Let's see if we can get online," I suggested. He shot me a look that said "Duh."

I'd never had a phone with Internet capability before, so it took a little getting used to. Especially since every time I lowered the phone enough to see what it was I was typing onto the screen, I lost the signal.

"Maybe we should walk this way a little bit," Logan said, pointing east. He held his phone in front of him in one hand and reached back to grab my hand in his other. "Watch your step."

It was a natural gesture, considerate, protective, just like when he took my hand in the hot springs. I'm pretty sure he didn't mean anything by it either time other than to be helpful, but that didn't stop the rush of pleasure that swelled up my arm and tingled in my stomach. I liked the feel of his hand, the way his fingers wrapped around mine, gentle, but firm, pulling, guiding—

Squish.

"Ha!" he laughed. "I told you to watch your step."

Lifting my foot gingerly, I wiped it along the clean dew-soaked (or rain-soaked) grass to clean off the boot. It was not a process that could be done with much dignity. Especially with Logan nearly doubled over next to me, laughing. One of the cows in the group on the hill lifted her head and mooed, as if she was laughing at me, too. So much for romantic gestures.

Logan helped me over the tall clumps of wet grass until we found a boulder sticking out from the hill that we could sit on. The sun had been shining on it just enough that the surface felt warm to the touch, but as soon as I sat down, the coolness beneath seeped through my jeans, and I shivered.

"Are you cold?" Logan asked. He didn't even wait for an answer but peeled off his jacket and handed it to me.

I murmured my thanks and wrapped the jacket around my shoulders.

Logan bent immediately over his phone, concentrating on moving things around the touch screen. I watched him quietly for a moment, smiling to myself. He could be annoying sometimes, but then he could be so considerate and genuine and sincere that it made my heart ache. I wondered again what he thought about our friendship.

Well, he was a guy, so he probably didn't think about it at all, but if he did, what would he think? Were we anything besides just really good friends? He almost kissed me once. Okay, *I* almost kissed *him* once, standing in the stairwell in Spain, right before he left. But he's the one who started it by hugging me. I thought I felt something from him then.

After that, there were the almost-nightly video chats. He wouldn't have spent all that time with me if he didn't like me, right? As more than a best friend, I mean.

And then what about in the lodge . . . that moment on the couch? If we hadn't noticed the blinking camera light that told us it was recording, would he have kissed me then?

As I looked at him, so unaware, bent over his phone, I got the feeling he was like the tree frog we'd seen hiding in that bromeliad. When we tried to look at it too closely, it had hopped away. Maybe it was the same with Logan. Maybe I should just be happy with the way things were and not try to define it, but just let it be.

Pura vida, I said to myself. And I understood a new layer of what it meant.

Logan must have felt me watching him, because he looked up at me then. "What?"

For an instant, I saw in my mind a flash of the colorful little frog skittering away, and I laughed. Yes, I had just compared Logan to a tree frog.

"What's so funny?" he demanded.

"Nothing," I said. "I was just thinking about something. You having any luck?"

"Well, I'm signed on," he said, and showed me his online status. "How about you?"

"Um, just a minute." I quickly found the right commands and navigated my way online.

"Can you sign in to your blog?" Logan asked.

"Oh." Well, that was one thing I couldn't do. "They've changed the passwords," I told him. "I'm supposed to submit my entries to someone at the network from now on, and they're going to post them."

"Well, we can look at it on the website anyway, to see if there's anything new." He typed in the URL. I did the same, trying to beat him. Our screens showed the *When in Rome* page at practically the same time. I hurried to manipulate the arrow and get to my blog. I beat him by half a breath. There had been no new entries since the two that I had removed the other day. Even my replacement post from the first day I had found a bogus message had been scrubbed. In its place were some pretty—but generic—pictures of Costa Rica. And the words: "Stay tuned for the next adventure." Clever.

"Looks like whatever they're doing is working," Logan said.

"Either that, or the hacker has lost interest," I said hopefully.

"Or, if we're right that it's someone here at the farm doing it, maybe they know we're on to them."

"Who do you think it is?" I asked.

"My lead suspect?" He thought for a moment. "Marco, probably."

"I don't know. He's been nice to us the whole time we've been here."

"He's too smooth," Logan said.

"What about Claudia?" I asked. "You can never tell what she's thinking. And she always seems to be watching us. It's eerie."

"Of course she's watching," Logan said. "She's a cameraman. Er, woman. And she's too obvious."

"What do you mean, obvious?"

"She's the most likely suspect, so it can't be her. Don't you ever watch crime shows?"

"Um, no. I don't really get a chance to watch much TV. How is it you do?"

"I didn't say I did." He raised his brows and smirked at me. Remember how I said he could be annoying? Yeah.

"So by your logic, our lead suspect has to be Estefan, because he's the least likely. He's so quiet and, I don't know . . . earnest."

"Earnest?"

"Yeah, like that time he was telling us about Monteverde's history, and he got all excited about—"

Logan grabbed my arm. "Wait. Look down there."

In the field below, Marco and Britt strolled along, hand in hand. Their voices carried up the hill, but not loud enough for us to understand what they were saying.

"Come on!" Logan said, pulling at me. "Hide."

We scrambled to the back of the rock and ducked behind it so that we could watch Britt and Marco, but hopefully they couldn't see us.

"Man, she's got it bad," Logan said.

Below, Britt was gazing up at Marco with such a stupid grin on her face, it was almost embarrassing to watch. Even more embarrassing, she giggled every few steps—that much carried clearly up the hill—and the two of them swung their hands back and forth like a lovey-dovey pendulum as they went along. I could just imagine their conversation: "I like you more." "No, I like you more." "Oh, no. I like you more." Blech. Unless it was Logan saying that to me . . .

They stopped to talk a little bit, and Britt threw her arms around Marco, then drew back and tucked her chin demurely, as if she couldn't believe what she had just done. Gag. He leaned in for the kiss, and I found myself holding my breath in anticipation. But then he planted one on her cheek. Wow. Mr. Romance.

Logan made a lovesick face and pantomimed kissing the air, and I laughed, then clapped my hand over my mouth to stifle the sound. Marco glanced up, and Logan and I dropped to the ground behind the boulder, trying not to laugh anymore. Of course, the harder we tried, the harder it was to keep it in. Logan's shoulders were moving up and down so fast, it looked like he was having a seizure. And my stomach shook until it ached.

"We better lie low until they're gone," Logan whispered, wiping his eyes.

I couldn't even answer, but nodded with my hand still clasped over my mouth.

Eventually, our laughter died down, and we settled onto the grass with our backs up against the warm/cold boulder. I closed my eyes and turned my face to the sun.

"I wonder how Victoria's doing," I said softly.

"I'm sure she's fine," he soothed.

"It looked pretty bad."

"Allergic reactions will do that. Once my cousin got stung by a bee, and his tongue swelled up so big he couldn't even swallow. They gave him a shot, and he was right as rain the next day."

I cracked one eye open and peeked at him, smiling. "Right as rain? Really?"

He bumped my shoulder with his. "Absolutely. Haven't you ever seen how right rain can be?"

I thought of huddling beneath the umbrella with Logan during the rain; hanging out with him inside because of the rain; dancing in the hot springs, our faces turned to the cooling rain. "Yeah," I said. "Yeah, I have."

I'm not sure how long we sat there together soaking in the sun, but finally, Logan said softly, "You think they're gone?"

I kind of hoped they weren't, because I liked being stuck with Logan. But I volunteered to check anyway. When I peeked around the edge of the stone, Britt and Marco were leaving, hands still swinging, near the far side of the field. "Almost," I told Logan.

He crawled around to where I was and looked for himself. "Where's he going?"

"What?" Okay, so I admit to being a little distracted, with Logan leaning around me to see down the hill, but I hadn't been paying attention. Britt was now heading toward the lodge, but Marco cut across the field toward the cow barn. At the door, he paused and checked furtively over each shoulder and then slipped inside. "All right. That was weird," I said.

"Looks like Marco has something to hide," Logan said darkly. "What did I say?"

I blew my bangs from my eyes. "Just because the man

went into the barn by himself doesn't mean he's our guy," I told him.

"He *snuck* into the barn," Logan corrected.

"Again, not proof of guilt."

"What do you think he's doing in there, milking cows?"

"He could be," I said stubbornly. "I'm sure there's plenty he could be doing to help out. My gramma says work is never done on a farm."

"But Marco's a *guide*," Logan said. "Why would he be working on the farm?"

I wouldn't back down. "Marco's *our* guide. That doesn't mean that's his occupation. Did you ever ask what he does when he's not showing us around?"

And on we went. We must have argued about Marco's true identity for about ten minutes before Logan stood and pointed to one of the rental SUVs making its way toward the road. "Hey, look. Someone's leaving."

"Who do you think it is? What if something's wrong with Victoria, and they called Liz to go to the hospital and—"

"Victoria is going to be fine. I keep telling you."

"Britt, then. What if she's gone looking for us?"

Logan rolled his eyes. "Stop worrying so much. Britt knows we went out to walk around the farm."

"Well, someone is leaving, and those are the only two grown-ups here from the group. Except Marco, and he's helping out in the barn."

"Hiding out in the barn," Logan said.

"Whatever. We should get back down there." I brushed off the seat of my pants—which had become uncomfortably damp from sitting on the ground—and had started down the hill when Logan stopped me.

"Uh, Cass? Look at this." He held his phone out to me, and I took it from his hand. On the screen was the logo for my blog, and beneath that . . . a new entry.

12

"What the—? When?" I sputtered. "We just looked at my blog half an hour ago and there was nothing here."

"Marco's been in that barn long enough to post something."

I couldn't believe it. But it looked like Logan was right. And I was wrong. I thought finding the hacker would make me feel powerful and vindicated, but in reality, it felt awful. Marco had been so nice to us. And to poor Britt . . . "Oh, my gosh," I breathed. "I know how he did it, how he found his way through the firewalls. Britt's our resident techie. He's been using her to get the information."

Logan scratched his cheek. "Why would she give it to him?"

"Are you kidding? She *likes* him. She probably didn't know what he was up to." My chest felt hollow thinking about it. "She's going to heartbroken."

"We've got to tell her," Logan said grimly.

"And Bayani and Victoria," I added.

"Let's go." He took my hand again to help me down the hill, and although I appreciated it (a lot), I was too upset to enjoy it the way I would have liked to.

By the time we burst into the lodge, I was completely out of breath. "Liz?" I wheezed. "Britt? Who's here?"

Mama Tica peeked out through the kitchen doorway, wiping her hands on a dish towel. "Hey! *Que pasa, cala*—" She stopped. "Is everything all right?"

"I need to talk to Liz," I said. "Do you know where she is?"

"You just missed her. One of my employees drove her down to the hospital."

"Oh, no!" I shot a look at Logan, as if Liz and the hospital were somehow his fault. Well, he did tell me I worried too much. "What's wrong?"

"Nothing bad," Mama Tica assured me. "There was some problem with the insurance, and the hospital needed a signature from your network representative."

Logan met my look with one that said "See?"

I ignored him. "Is Britt around?" I asked.

"She said she was going to find you," Mama Tica said. "Have you been playing hide-and-seek?"

"We went for a walk," Logan volunteered.

Mama Tica hid a smile. "Yes, there is a lot of walking going on these days."

I stole a quick peek at Logan, hoping he didn't catch her meaning. Britt and Marco's walks were all about romance. She probably thought Logan's and mine was, too. Not that I wouldn't have liked that. I think. But I didn't want Logan to get embarrassed. Okay, and I didn't want to be embarrassed, either.

"We should find Britt," I told Logan.

"She was out by the car shed last time I saw her," Mama Tica said.

I thanked her, and Logan and I ran back outside.

"There you are!" Britt called when saw us. "I've been looking all over for you."

"Sorry." I looked around to make sure Marco wasn't within earshot and then asked if she knew what time everyone else was getting back.

She seemed to catch the urgency in my voice and was suddenly concerned. "Why? What's wrong?"

I looked to Logan, unsure of how much to say. He made the decision for me. "We know who's been hacking into Cassidy's blog," he said.

"We've got to talk to Bayani," I added.

Britt shook her head as if she hadn't heard right. "What are you talking about?"

"We saw . . ." I floundered and looked to Logan for help again. "I can't say it."

He took over for me. "Whoever was posting those things on Cassidy's blog has been doing it from right here," he said. "Bayani's friend tracked it for us."

"I was sure it was Claudia," I told her.

"But it wasn't." Logan stalled, and I'm sure he felt as awkward delivering the news to her as I did. He took a deep breath and then finished in a rush, "It was Marco."

We probably could have blown a puff of air at her and knocked her right over. "M-Marco?" she repeated.

"We saw him," I said, finally finding my voice, "sneaking into the barn. And then a few minutes later, another post showed up on my blog, even though the passwords have all been changed and . . . and . . ." I let my words die off because Britt's face had gone completely white. I couldn't even imagine how she must be feeling—especially if Marco had milked any of the tech information out of her.

She shook her head. "I don't believe it. Why are you saying this? It's impossible. There's not even an Internet connection here."

"But there's supposed to be a connection," I said. "We think somehow he's been jamming it."

"Then how," she demanded, "could you have seen anything he posted?"

"Our phones," Logan said. "You can get a signal up the

hill. That's how we saw him. We were up on the hill trying to find the signal, and—"

"We're sorry, Britt," I told her. "We really are."

She crossed her arms tight across her chest, which anyone knows is a defensive gesture. I felt so bad for her. "What now?" she asked, her voice small and lost.

"We need to tell Bayani," Logan said, "and have his friend verify that this last post came from here so we can prove it was Marco. Then we can take it to the network, and with luck we can win back the sponsors and save our show."

Just then, I saw Marco on the path coming from the barn. I nudged Logan, and he gestured to Britt. When she saw Marco, she staggered back a step.

When she turned back to Logan and me, her lips were pressed into a grim line, and her nostrils flared. I've never seen anyone go from heartbroken to angry so quickly. "Let's go," she said. "I'll take you to Bayani."

Marco called out to her and waved. "Hurry," she urged, and herded us to the car shed.

"Hey," Marco called. "Hey, Britt!"

She wrenched open the door of the remaining rental SUV and hissed to us, "Get in. Quickly."

Logan and I scrambled into the backseat just seconds before Britt threw the thing into reverse and squealed out of the shed. Through the rear window, I could see Marco running toward us, waving his arms and shouting.

"Go! Go!" I yelled.

Britt shifted into drive before the SUV had completely stopped and the gears ground angrily before they caught, pitching us forward. She sped down the driveway and swung out onto the road, mumbling to herself the whole way.

In the backseat, Logan and I were tossed first one way and then the other. "Seat belt," he told me, and pulled his own over his shoulder and lap. The SUV bounced and shuddered over the potholes.

"Um, Britt?" I reached forward to nudge her shoulder, but I was thrown back by another door-rattling bump in the road. "We're clear. You can slow down now."

She slammed on the brakes, and Logan and I were thrown forward. I was grateful he had reminded me to strap in. "Sorry," she sniffed. "I'm so sorry."

Logan and I sat quietly in the backseat and left her to her thoughts and her tears. What could we say? I couldn't think of anything that would make her feel better, so I kept my mouth shut.

Until we veered off the main road just before we reached town. The new road was narrower and paved with gravel that spit and pinged against the underside of the car so that I had to yell over the noise. "Where are we going?"

"To the hospital, to see Bayani," she yelled back.

The SUV bucked and rattled down the road. I mean literally *down* the road. As in, we were headed downhill.

I wondered where the hospital was. I couldn't think of another town close to Monteverde except for Santa Elena, and that seemed to be *across* from Monteverde, not down.

We had gone maybe five miles before the SUV began to sputter and slow until finally Britt pulled over to the side of the road and we lurched to a stop.

"I do not believe this," she muttered. "The thing's overheated."

"We're stuck?" I asked stupidly.

She turned around in her seat. "Do either of you know anything about engines?"

We both shook our heads.

"Great." She popped the hood and kicked open her door to climb out.

"Maybe we should see if we can help," I said to Logan.

We joined Britt at the front of the car to frown at the engine parts.

"It will be okay," Britt told us. "The radiator needs water so it can cool off."

"Do we have any water in the car?" I asked helpfully.

"No, but there are some empty drink cups in the front-seat holders," Britt said. "Maybe you and Logan could climb down to that stream and fill them up."

Logan and I looked toward the swollen stream at the bottom of the embankment, and then at each other and shrugged. Sounded like as good an idea as any. We grabbed the cups and started climbing down the hill, which is much easier than it sounds, because we were still wearing those silly rubber boots, so we had no traction on the loose rocks and kept slipping and skidding down the embankment.

We were only about halfway down when I heard the engine turn over again. "Logan. Listen. She got it started." We scrambled back up to find that Britt had turned the car around so that it was facing up the road.

She rolled the window down and called out to us. "I'm sorry, kids! I didn't want to have to do this, but you couldn't leave well enough alone. Just follow this road uphill and you'll find the road that leads to Monteverde. You can call your parents from there."

"What are you doing?" Logan demanded.

"Leaving Monteverde it appears, thanks to you."

I dropped my empty cup. "I don't understand."

"That's fine," she said. "You will in time. But by then, my post on your blog will have done its work, and I will be long gone."

"*Your* post on my blog?" I sputtered. "What are you talking about?"

"My job."

"Your job? But . . . you work for the show. You're one of us."

"Right," she said with a sneer. "You keep believing that."

Her foot came off the brake, and the SUV started to roll forward.

"Where are you going?" I asked.

She laughed. "Do you really think I'd be foolish enough to tell you?"

During the exchange, Logan kept inching forward, closer to the car. I had to keep her talking.

"So it was you this whole time?" I could see how it was possible. She was our computer wiz. Even if she didn't know the new website passwords and firewall protection, she could probably get around them. "But why?"

She wasn't going to fall for it. "Love to stick around and chat," she called, "but I have to eat some road before you call in the cavalry. Ta-ta!"

And with that, she gunned it, leaving a cloud of dust in her wake and Logan running after her. Finally, he saw it was futile and let her go.

"I'm sorry," he said. "I tried."

I ran up to where he had bent over, resting his hands on his knees as he struggled to catch his breath. "It's okay," I said. "Everything's going to be fine."

He shook his head. "No. It's not," he puffed. "I let her get away."

"Not quite."

He straightened up and looked at me, his brows drawn. "What?"

"Didn't you notice how weird she was acting?" I asked. "I was already starting to get bad vibes when she turned off of the main road, but that whole thing about sending us down the hill to fetch a cup of water? Too cute. So I tucked my phone into her purse. It's got that GPS tracker on it. Wherever she goes, we'll know it."

Logan's face broke into a huge smile. "Well played, Barnett, well played."

"You still have your phone with you, right?" I asked.

"Yeah," he said, "but I don't know if we can get a signal all the way out—"

"Um," I cut in, "I also noticed one of those 'camouflaged' cell-phone towers back up the road a way. We should get a pretty strong signal from here if you want to call your dad or Bayani to come pick us up."

"Excellent!" Logan high-fived me and then pulled out his phone to tell his dad what happened, and to give him directions where to find us.

We started walking up the hill toward the main road, and Logan reached back for my hand to pull me along, even though I was less than half a step behind him. Maybe it wasn't to pull me then? Maybe all these times he was holding my hand because he wanted to *hold my hand*. Again, I wished I could think of how to ask him. How to tell him what I felt. But it was easier just to slip my hand in his and go with it. I smiled to myself. *Pura vida*.

"What is it?" Logan asked.

I blinked at him. "What?"

"You and your looks and your secret smiles. Is there something I should know?"

My cheeks felt hotter than the Arenal springs, and I just

about pulled my hand away from his, but he held on tight. "Nothing," I said. "It's nothing." Nothing that I could find the words to tell him anyway.

He stopped in the middle of the road. "And you say I'm annoying! There's something you're not telling me. So spill."

I should have been able to tell him then, but I was still afraid. What if he didn't feel the same about me? What if it ruined our friendship?

"I was thinking about that cute little tree frog," I said finally. "You know how you have to be still or it might hop away? So even though you want to look closer, you can't. You just have to let it be."

"Yes?" he asked.

What did he mean? That was it. Didn't he understand? It had sounded really deep to me when I was thinking about it in the south pasture. I sighed. "Well, you're the frog."

He threw his head back and laughed. "That's what I like about you, Cass," he said. "You always say the craziest things."

I forced my lips into a smile. "You know it. *La chica moda*, always good for a laugh."

Travel tip: Once you visit Costa Rica,

it is hard to leave. . . .

So what happened next? Zoe texted.

Britt gave the investigators a full confession, I wrote.

Not that Britt had intended on giving one. Turns out I did learn a thing or two from being on a reality show. Before sticking my phone into her purse, I turned on the video recorder. It didn't get pictures of anything besides the satin lining of her purse, but it did pick up everything she yelled to Logan and me before she left us stranded. Confronted with the evidence, Britt quickly broke down and confessed.

Why did she do it? Zoe asked.

You know that show *A Foreign Affair*? They're kind of a rival of my mom and dad's show.

I have seen that one, Zoe texted. And . . . ?

Britt said someone from *A Foreign Affair* hired her to sabotage *When in Rome*, I answered. She lost our luggage, ditched supplies, destroyed entire segments of film. And, of course, hacked into my blog to scare off the sponsors and prevent *When in Rome* from branching out.

That is not nice, Zoe said, texting the obvious. You are angry about this?

I thought about that for a moment. Was I angry? In a way, yes. But in the long run, what did it matter?

Zoe, I typed, have I ever told you about the Costa Rican motto of pura vida?

Not surprisingly, the production company behind *A Foreign Affair* denied even knowing Britt, let alone hiring her to go after our show. In fact, they went a step further, actually accusing my mom and dad of manufacturing the entire scenario to try to bring down *A Foreign Affair*. Ironically, the more the fight played out in the tabloids, the higher the ratings got for each show. The only one left out of the limelight was Britt.

It would have been a great ending to the trip if the sponsors who had dumped us had rushed to sign back up after we solved our hacking mystery, but unfortunately, that's not what happened. A couple of them had already moved on to sponsor other projects, and one was still spooked by the idea that something like this could happen again—even though Cavin and Liz had both assured them that it wouldn't.

That's okay, though, because once the tabloids picked up the story (you knew they would), a handful of other sponsors lined up to take their places.

If only my mom and dad could be so easily charmed by a happy outcome.

"It was smart thinking at the end," Mom said, "but you should never have gotten yourself into that situation in the first place."

"You could have gotten hurt," Dad said. "Or worse."

And even though it just about killed me not to try to explain or to offer excuses, I told them, "You're right. I'm very sorry."

I think my apology surprised them so much that they forgot to decide on a punishment for me.

Mama Tica told me later that she was proud of the way I had handled myself and that I will have a happy life if I continue to think *pura vida*.

● ● ● ● ●

On our last day in Costa Rica, the whole crew went to the airport together, and we saw each flight off one by one until it was time to say good-bye to Victoria.

"I'm so glad you were able to be cleared for your flight," Mom told her. "I was worried about your foot."

"Ach, she's fine," Cavin scoffed. "Just an allergic reaction."

"Yes, but it looks quite uncomfortable," Mom said. I could have told Mom that Victoria never let being uncomfortable stop her.

Sure enough, Victoria insisted that her foot wasn't that bad. "Truly. I don't require this wheelchair."

Dad chuckled. "Stay put for one more minute. You can hobble around all you want once we get you to your gate."

"I do not hobble," Victoria muttered.

Logan hid a laugh, but not quick enough.

"Enjoy the break," Victoria told him. "You and Cassidy still owe me completed research papers. I will expect them online within the week."

We waved Victoria off, and she walked onto her plane. Now all that were left were Logan and his dad and my mom and dad and me. Our flight was the last one scheduled to leave; theirs was second to last.

Logan turned to face me, and suddenly, I was tongue-tied. The whole morning I had been listing in my head the things Logan and I should say to each other before we went our different ways, but I couldn't remember any of it now that he was just moments away from leaving.

In fact, a very few moments. Cavin checked the monitor, and his eyes sprang open wide. "*Orra*, look at the time! Our flight's about to board."

"Quickly, then," Mom urged, and herded us toward the end of the concourse, where Logan and his dad's gate was.

I jogged beside Logan, trying to remember all the right things to say for good-bye. Nothing came except small talk. "So you'll be staying with your mom over the break?" I asked him. We wouldn't start shooting the next show until after Christmas.

"Yeah. And you're at your grandmum's?"

"Yep." We'd already been over our holiday plans about ten times, so this didn't really count as conversation.

A woman's voice came over the loudspeaker, "Now preboarding all first-class, business, and medallion passengers on flight twelve ninety-two, bound for Dublin, Ireland."

"Are you medallion?" I asked.

He nodded.

Shoot, shoot, shoot. I couldn't think. Cavin was picking up his carry-on and sliding the strap over his shoulder.

"Cassidy," Logan began.

"I know," I said, panicked. "You have to leave, but—"

"Logan," Cavin said. "It's time."

I took a deep breath. I was just going to say it. Just tell him, and not worry about the consequences. *Pura vida.* "Logan," I said, at the same time that he said, "Cassidy."

"Go ahead," I told him. Disappointed. Relieved.

"All right, son," Cavin said, patting Logan on the shoulder. "Let's go."

"Just a sec, Da."

"It's time now."

"I'll talk to you soon, okay?" Logan said. He turned to walk away.

"Wait!" I called after him. He looked back at me expectantly. Words! Where were the words?

I ran after him to give him a hug instead. He hugged me back for probably half a second. What did you expect with our parents standing there, looking on?

"Thanks," he said, smiling.

"Uh-huh," I mumbled.

Cavin dragged Logan toward the check-in. "Bye, Cass," Logan called.

"Bye!" I stepped back and watched him walk away. He turned and waved one last time before disappearing down the Jetway, and then he was gone.

I should have been disappointed. I mean, I hadn't worked up the nerve to tell Logan what I felt. But the irony was, after all that worrying about what to say, it wasn't the words that mattered after all. What mattered was what was real.

"All righty, then, Cassie-bug," Dad said. "Are you ready to go home?"

"Yes," I told him. "Yes, I am."

Epilogue

Gramma brought a mug of hot cocoa out to the screened porch where I sat watching dry leaves skitter across the empty rows in the garden. The soil had been turned over for the winter and wouldn't see vegetables again until spring.

"You ready to come in?" Gramma asked, handing me the mug. "Wind's picking up. It's fixing to get cold."

I wrapped my fingers around the warm ceramic. "Just a little longer," I told her.

She clucked like an old mother hen but didn't say anything more. By now she probably knew it was a lost cause. I'd spent a lot of my days sitting out on the porch reading, working on my home-study homework, but mostly just staring out over the property. I kept seeing another barn, another pasture, another stand of trees.

Gramma turned to go back inside, but before she closed the door, she paused. "Your mother and daddy will be back from town in just a bit. We'll eat supper as soon as they get here."

I pulled my jacket tighter and nodded. "Thanks for the hot chocolate, Gramma." Eventually, the door latch clicked shut and I was alone again.

It had been three weeks since we'd left Costa Rica. Three weeks without a word from Logan. I had tried texting him, calling him, IMing, too, but he still hadn't answered. I shouldn't have been surprised; he'd done this once before— going silent for two years before surfacing again in Spain. The difference was, I thought we had a connection in Costa Rica. Saying good-bye to him in the airport, I thought I knew what was "real." Now I wasn't so sure anymore.

That's why I kept wishing I was back at Mama Tica's farm. The afternoon Logan and I hiked to the pasture was about as perfect as you could get. Until that whole Britt-kidnapping-us thing, I mean.

In the past week, three of the mini episodes Logan and I had filmed in Costa Rica had aired on TV, but I couldn't make myself watch any of them. Was it all pretend, like Logan said? Had I imagined everything I thought I felt in Monteverde? Dad kept telling me that our little shows were very popular, and I should have been happy about that, but it really didn't matter to me. Not much anyway.

I mean, as long as people liked the shows, the sponsors were happy. And if the sponsors were happy, our shows would continue. Which meant Logan and I would be working together again. I just couldn't decide how to feel about that.

Inside, I heard my parents' voices. I sipped on my cocoa and counted, waiting for Gramma to call me in for supper. She made it to the door before I got to eleven.

I trudged in behind her, feeling tragic, until I got to the kitchen table and Dad handed me a small brown package. The return address was Dublin, Ireland. "We picked this up at the post office," he said. "Who do you suppose it's from?"

"Ha-ha." Cradling the package, I turned my back on him and slipped outside to the porch, where I ripped through the brown paper. Inside was a small box with a shiny red bow. A note fluttered to the ground, and I bent to pick it up.

"Happy Christmas, Cass. I noticed you never got a chance to get a charm for your necklace in Costa Rica. This reminded me of you. I figured you'd know what it meant."

I tore off the bright paper and flipped open the lid.

And stopped.

Inside, nestled on a square of cotton, was a round wooden charm inlaid with a tiny gold tree frog.

Fingers trembling, I undid my necklace and tied the charm onto the leather cord. Hooking the clasp behind my neck again, I smoothed the charms down, my fingers running over the smooth shape of the frog.

Once I had compared Logan to a tree frog, afraid to look at his friendship too closely for fear it might go away. Now he had given me a symbol of a tree frog to keep with me forever.

Funny how a few seconds can change your perspective. Suddenly, I didn't care about the weeks of silence since I left Logan in Costa Rica. All I could think about now was the remaining weeks ahead before I would see him again.

When? Zoe asked when I texted her that evening.

Just after the first of the year, I typed. **I can't wait.**

Where did you say you were going again?

I smiled, already seeing in my mind's eye Logan and me hand in hand among the kangaroos and koalas.

Australia, I texted. **Next time I see Logan, it will be in Australia.**

TURN THE PAGE FOR A PEEK AT

LIGHTS, CAMERA,
CASSIDY

EPISODE ONE:
Celebrity

I like a challenge.

My grampa used to say my determination was something that could get me far in life. What he didn't say was that it could also get me in trouble.

I found out just how much trouble the night I snuck out of our apartment in Spain.

The tabloids have printed at least a hundred different versions of what happened next. Some of the stories are true. Most of them, not so much. I still have to laugh that the papers ran them at all.

I mean, since when am *I* news? First of all, I'm only twelve (almost thirteen). Second, before Spain, hardly anyone even knew who I was. No, I take that back. They might have seen my picture on one of those celebrity shows or in a magazine, but never just as me. I was always an accessory, an extension of my parents—*Cassidy Barnett, daughter of reality TV stars Julia and Davidson Barnett.*

See, my mom and dad host a travel show called *When in Rome.* Not only that, but my mom has written about ten international cookbooks and my dad has his own line of travel accessories. Until Spain, my only job was to jet around the world with them, watching from the sideline. Hardly anyone ever noticed me.

But then everything changed.

What happened that first morning wasn't my fault. Well, okay, it sort of was, but none of it would have happened if the airline hadn't lost my suitcase, so at least partial blame belongs to them.

The way I see it, I wouldn't have had to sneak out if I could have set up my room properly. I'm not talking about full-on decor or anything, just a few things I bring with me when we travel. We move around with the show so much that I could easily end up sleeping in a strange bed in a strange room every few weeks. Having my stuff set up helps make each room feel like *mine.*

I have a brass incense burner I bought in India, a string of star-shaped twinkling lights from France, a fuzzy Japanese Hello Kitty pillow, and—most importantly—a framed picture of my grampa and me that was taken at his farm in Ohio.

That picture was the last one we ever had taken together. We're sitting on the creaky old porch swing in front of his house, and Grampa's smiling straight into the camera like he knows he's going to be looking out at me from the other side. I can almost hear him telling me, "Wherever you go, Cassie, I'll be there with you."

But he wasn't there that first morning in Valencia, all because of the stupid airline.

It was still dark outside when I woke up. At first, everything was fine. I lay in bed and listened to the pipes knocking in the walls, imagining all the places we were going to visit for the show that day.

Then I remembered. I had no suitcase. The cute new sundress I'd bought to wear for my first day in Spain was lost in some airport somewhere. Worse, without my things, my room felt empty. Empty. EMPTY.

I switched on the lamp to chase away the shadows, but—even with its authentic Mediterranean touches—the room looked even bleaker in the light . . . like a really well-furnished cell. The air smelled stale. The closeness of the walls made my skin itch. I couldn't stand it. I had to get *out*. Out of the room, out of the apartment, out of the building so I could breathe again.

The problem was, my mom and dad were still asleep,

and it would have been rude to wake them up just to ask for permission, right? I wasn't going to go far. Maybe just walk around our temporary neighborhood a little bit. Explore the surroundings. We were staying right in the middle of the historic district, so I could probably get some good pictures for my blog—even if it was still kind of dark.

Did I mention it was four in the morning?

The early hour would make slipping out a little tricky. My mom and dad's bedroom was right across the hall from mine. Plus, there was a doorman on duty down in the lobby who might ask questions. But as I said, I like a challenge. I figured I was up for it.

That was my first mistake.

Getting out of the apartment was easy. My mom and dad aren't exactly known for being light sleepers. Which was good because my dad snores loud enough to drown out a 747. They probably didn't even hear me tiptoe past their room and out the front door of the apartment.

Sneaking down to the lobby was the tricky part. The elevator was one of those really old cagelike things that rattled and groaned whenever it went up and down. If I didn't want to wake up everyone in the building, I had to take the stairs, and that meant I had zero chance of getting past the doorman unnoticed. The staircase emptied out right in front of his desk.

Sure enough, I got only about halfway down the steps before he glanced up from the soccer game he was watching on the small television at his desk. From his bland expression, I couldn't tell if he recognized me or not. Like I said, my mom and dad were the television stars. I was just a footnote. But he had to know I belonged with the Americans who had arrived that night. If he wanted to rat me out, he'd know exactly who to buzz, so I had to make sure he didn't think there was a reason to rat.

I gave him my best celebrity smile and practically sang "Good morning!" as I bounced down the rest of the stairs.

"Buenos días," he replied, but he didn't smile back. His heavy black eyebrows huddled together like he was unsure what he was supposed to do next. He kind of half stood, stooped over, like a question mark hanging in the air.

I pointed to myself and then to the revolving glass front door. "Going running."

His face relaxed, and he settled back into his seat like I figured he would.

See, the thing about most grown-ups is that they would rather not know if something's wrong because then they have to deal with it. So as long as I acted like it was perfectly normal for someone my age to go out running alone before the sun came up, it was a pretty good bet he wouldn't bother me. Or alert my mom and dad. Or notice that I was wearing purple Converse high-tops, not running shoes.

I breezed through the lobby, waving good-bye to the

doorman as I passed his desk, but he had already turned back to his game.

Once I was safely outside and down the block—out of sight of the apartment building—I paused to pull my cell phone and earbuds from my pocket. I quickly put together a playlist of Spanish music that ran exactly thirty-four minutes. That way, when I got to the last song, I would know it was time to turn back. Just to be safe, I also set the phone's alarm so I'd be sure to make it to the apartment before the time Mom and Dad usually woke up.

After all that, I finally relaxed. I closed my eyes and took a deep breath, savoring the smell of freedom and Valencia. I know that probably sounds weird, but every city has its own smell—especially in the morning before it gets buried under exhaust fumes and heat. In Valencia it was a combination of concrete and oranges and fresh-cut grass, with a faint, salty sea tang that drifted in with the mist from the ocean. I made a mental note of it, and set off to find some pictures to post as well.

I started my blog when my grampa first got sick. Because his medicine made him feel tired a lot, he had to stop driving and he couldn't do as much around the farm as he used to. I hated that while my mom and dad and I were off seeing the world with the show, his world was shrinking. Gramma finally got wireless at the house and bought him a laptop so he could sit out on the porch and still be able to get online. It helped for him to have something to keep his mind occupied, she said.

I had just gotten a new cell phone with a camera from my mom and dad for my birthday, so I decided to keep a photo diary of our travels for Grampa. That way he'd have some kind of connection with us whenever he got online. I wrote him notes and took pictures I thought would make him laugh. Like Dad asleep on the plane with a big string of drool hanging from his mouth. Or Mom prepping for a segment with rollers in her hair and the makeup tissue tucked into her collar.

When Grampa died, I kept the blog going. It made me feel like I was still connected to him in a way. I continued to send him messages and talk to him as if he was with me. I kept looking for things I knew would make him smile.

It didn't take long before fans of my mom and dad's show discovered my blog. When the *When in Rome* producers saw how many followers I was getting, they offered to host my blog on their website. They even bought me a nicer cell phone with a better camera—this one with video. That should have been my first clue that the blog wasn't just about Grampa anymore.

Within weeks, my hundreds of followers turned into thousands. Mom and Dad weren't thrilled to have so many strangers following me, even if most of those followers were fans of the show. After a long discussion with the network, it was decided I could keep blogging as long as I followed a strict list of guidelines, which included disabling the comments. The last thing my mom and dad wanted was some creeper talking to me online.

So anyway, that's how it all started. I'll admit that when I snuck out that morning, it did occur to me that just in case I wound up getting caught, my mom and dad might go easier on me if I could say I'd done it all for the blog. Proves how much I know.

Our apartment building sat across the street from the Plaza de la Reina, which put us within walking distance of everything in Old Town—the Turia Fountain, the basilica, and the Valencia Cathedral with its *miguelete* tower.

I wandered through the historic district, mostly just getting background images that I would edit later when I wrote about our first day in Spain.

Hardly anyone was out that morning, only a few cars going through the roundabout and maybe a delivery truck or two. It was peaceful and quiet as I walked along—just me and my camera and the music.

The last song in my playlist was just ending as I reached the Plaza de la Virgen. I checked the time. Close. I quickly tucked away the earbuds and set the camera to video. The plaza had its own music in the sloshing of the fountain and a quartet of birds too impatient to wait for dawn. It was the perfect sound track for a quick vlog message to go along with all the images I'd been filming.

I propped my phone on the edge of the fountain, making the Door of the Apostles and the Valencia Cathedral my backdrop, and took a few steps back.

"*Buenos días, Abuelo,*" I said to the camera. "That means 'Good morning, Grampa.' We got to Spain late last night, but—"

Just then my phone started to vibrate, buzzing and skipping over the stones toward the pool of the fountain.

"Crap!" I jumped and managed to grab the phone right before it fell into the water. My heart felt like it was going to pound its way right out of my chest. The alarm meant I had to get back to the apartment. Fast.

I held the phone at arm's length and finished quickly. "I've got to run, but I'll give you an update later. *¡Nos vemos pronto!* That's Spanish for 'See you soon.' *¡Adios!*"

The doorman was standing behind his desk when I rushed back into the lobby. He'd been talking on the phone, but he cut it short and set down the receiver when he saw me. His little television wasn't on anymore.

Oh, crap, I thought. *He knows I snuck out.*

Dread clawed at me every step up the staircase to our apartment. If the door guy knew I wasn't supposed to be out on my own, someone must have told him. Someone like my mom and dad. They were probably waiting for me on the landing, ready to lock me in my room. I trudged even slower.

The door to our apartment was silent and closed, just the way I'd left it. Maybe all wasn't lost. I pulled the key from my pocket and reached for the door when a shape stepped out from the shadows.

"Oooh. You're in trouble."

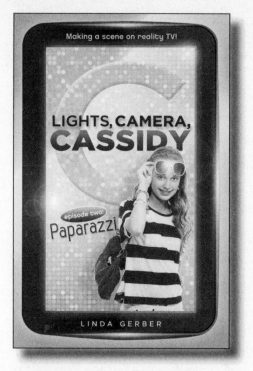

ISBN: 978-0-14-241815-4

Cassidy has a fabulous opportunity to be in an upcoming travelogue about the Greek Isles. For the show, she will be living on board a swank yacht and be hosted by a wealthy local actor and his adorable son, Nikos. But Cass soon starts to suspect that things aren't really as they seem on the *Pandora*. At the same time, she wonders what's going on with Logan—he hasn't been around for their nightly e-chats. Can she find out the truth about the *Pandora*? And can she get her relationship with Logan back on track—before it's too late?

LOOK FOR...

EPISODE FOUR:
Drama

COMING SOON!

Get Hooked
ON THESE OTHER
FABULOUS
Girl Series!

Lucy B. Parker: Girl vs. Superstar
By Robin Palmer
AVAILABLE NOW!

Forever Four
By Elizabeth Cody Kimmel
AVAILABLE NOW!

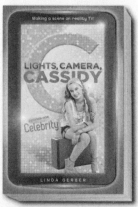

Lights, Camera, Cassidy: Episode 1: Celebrity
By Linda Gerber
AVAILABLE NOW!

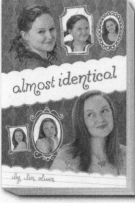

Almost Identical
By Lin Oliver

Check out sample chapters at
http://tinyurl.com/penguingirlsampler

Grosset & Dunlap • Puffin Books • Divisions of Penguin Young Readers Group
www.penguin.com/youngreaders